John Bunyan, Samuel Phillips Day, Frederick Barnard, M.
Paolo Priolo

Bunyan's Pilgrim's Progress

in words of one syllable

John Bunyan, Samuel Phillips Day, Frederick Barnard, M. Paolo Priolo

Bunyan's Pilgrim's Progress
in words of one syllable

ISBN/EAN: 9783337291259

Printed in Europe, USA, Canada, Australia, Japan

Cover: Foto ©Andreas Hilbeck / pixelio.de

More available books at **www.hansebooks.com**

IN·WORDS·OF·ONE·SYLLABLE
PILGRIM'S
PROGRESS

At last there came a grave man to the gate, whose name was Goodwill.

(Page 13)   *(The Pilgrim's Progress.)*

BUNYAN'S

PILGRIM'S PROGRESS.

IN WORDS OF ONE SYLLABLE.

By SAMUEL PHILLIPS DAY,

AUTHOR OF "THE RARE ROMANCE OF REYNARD THE FOX," IN WORDS OF ONE SYLLABLE.

ILLUSTRATED.

A. L. BURT COMPANY,
PUBLISHERS,   NEW YORK.

THE
PILGRIM'S PROGRESS.

CHAPTER I.

THE DEN AND THE DREAM.

As I went through the wilds of this world, I came to a place where was a den, and I laid me down in that place to sleep; and as I slept I dreamt a dream; and lo, I saw a man clad in rags, with a book in his hand, and a great load on his back! I saw him read in the book, and as he read, he wept and shook.

In this plight, then, he went home, and kept calm as long as he could, that his wife and bairns should not see his grief; but he could not long hold his speech, for that his woe grew more hard to bear. "Oh, my dear wife," said he, "and you, the bairns of my heart, I am quite lost, for a load lies hard on me. More than this, I am told that this our town will be burnt with fire from the skies, and you, my sweet babes, shall come to grief, save some way can be found to get clear of harm." At this his kin were in sore fear; for that they had just cause to dread some dire ill had got hold of his head. So, when morn was come, they would know how he did: and he told them,

"Worse and worse." He spoke to them once more, but they gave no heed to his words. Hence he went to his room to pray for them, and to ease his grief. He would, too, take long walks in the fields, and read and pray at times: and thus for some days he spent his time.

Now I saw on a time, when he took a stray walk in the fields, that he was bent on his book and in deep grief of mind; and as he read he burst out, "What shall I do?"

I saw, too, that his eyes went this way and that way, as if he would run: yet he could not tell which way to go. I then saw a man whose name was Evangelist come to him and ask, "Why dost thou cry?" Quoth he, "Sir, I see by the book in my hand that death is my doom, and that I am then to meet my Judge: and I find that I do not will to do the first, while I dread the last." Then said Evangelist, "Why not will to die, since this life is full of ills?" The man said, "The cause is I fear that this load that is on my back will sink me more low than the grave, and I shall go down to hell."

Then said Evangelist, "If this be thy state, why dost thou stand still?" Said he, "It is for that I know not where to go." Then he gave him a roll of smooth skin, on which were writ the plain words, "Flee from the wrath to come." The man read it, and said, "To what place must I flee?" Then said Evangelist, "Do you see yon small gate?" The man said, "I think I do." Then said his guide, "Go up at once to it; at which, when thou dost knock, it shall be told thee what thou shalt do."

So I saw in my dream that the man did run. Now he had not run far from his own door, but his wife and bairns saw it, and in a loud voice they strove to get him to come back; but the man put the tips of his thumbs in his ears and ran on.

His friends also came out, and some **bade him** haste
back. Of those who did so, there were two that sought to
fetch him back by force. The name of the one was Obstinate; and the name of the next, Pliable. Now by this
time the man was a good way off; but they went in quest
of him, and in a short time came up with him. Then said

OBSTINATE GOES BACK TO THE CITY OF DESTRUCTION.

he, "Friends, for what are ye come?" Quoth they, "To
urge you to go back with us": but he said, "That can by
no means be. You dwell in the City of Destruction: and
when you die there, you will sink down to a place that
burns with fire. Take heed, good friends, and go with me."

"What!" said Obstinate, "and leave **our** friends and
all that brings us joy and ease?"

"Yes," said Christian (for that was his name) ; "I seek a life that fades not. Read it so, if you will, in my book."

"Tush!" said Obstinate, "I heed not your book : will you go back with us or no?"

"No, not I," said Christian.

Obs.—"Come then, friend Pliable, let us go home."

Then said Pliable, "The things he looks for are of more worth than ours. My heart urges me to go with him."

Obs.—"What! Be led by me and go back."

Chr.—"Come with me, friend Pliable; there are such things to be had which I spoke of, and much more bliss. If you heed not what I say, read here in this book."

"Well, friend Obstinate," said Pliable, "I mean to go with this good man, and to cast in my lot with him. But, my good mate, do you know the way to this place?"

Chr.—"I am told by a man, whose name is Evangelist, to speed me to a small gate that is in front of us, where we shall be put in the right way."

"And I will go back to my place," said Obstinate. "I will not make one of such flat fools."

CHAPTER II.

THE SLOUGH OF DESPOND.

Now Christian and Pliable spoke as they did walk on the plain; and this was what they said :

Chr.—"Come, friend Pliable. I am glad you have been led to go with me. Had but Obstinate felt what I have felt, he would not have set his back on us."

Pli.—"And do you think that your book is true?"

Chr.—"Yes: there is a realm where we shall not taste of death, that we may dwell in it for aye."

Pli.—" This is right good; and what else ? "

Chr.—" There we shall not weep or grieve more ; for he that owns the place will wipe all tears from our eyes."

Pli.—" To hear this doth fill one's heart with joy. But are these things to form our bliss ? How shall we get to share in them ? "

Chr.—" The Lord hath set down *that* in this book, the pith of which is, if we in truth seek to have it, he will, of his free grace, grant it to us."

Pli.—" Well, my good friend, glad am I to hear of these things. Come on, let us mend our pace."

Now I saw in my dream that just as they had put an end to this talk they drew up nigh to a deep slough that was in the midst of the plain ; and as they did not heed it, both fell swap in the bog. The name of the slough was Despond.

Then said Pliable, " Ah, friend Christian, where are you now ? "

" In sooth," said Christian, " I do not know."

At this Pliable said in sharp tones, " Is this the bliss you have told me all this while of ? If we have such ill speed as we first set out, what may we not look for ere the time we get to the end of our road ? May I once get out with my life, you shall hold the brave land for me." And with that he gave a bold stride or two, and got out of the mire on that side of the slough which was next his own house. So off he went, and Christian saw him no more.

Hence Christian was left to sprawl in the Slough of Despond. But I saw in my dream that a man came to him whose name was Help, and did ask him what he did there.

" Sir," said Christian, " I was bade go this way by a man

known as **Evangelist**, who sent me in like way to yon gate, that I might scape the wrath to come."

So he gave him his hand, and drew him out, and set him on sound ground, and let him go on his way.

Then I went to him that did pluck him out, and said, "Sir, whence is it that this plat is not made whole, that those who pass this way may run no risk ?"

And he said to me, "This slough is such a place that none can mend it. It goes by the name of the Slough of Despond ; for still, as he who sins is wrought up to a sense of his lost state, there spring forth in his soul fears, and doubts, and dark thoughts that scare, which all of them form in a heap and fix in this place ; and this is the cause why the road is so bad. True, there are, by the help of him who frames the laws, some stout and firm steps found through the midst of this slough ; these steps are all but hid, or if they be seen, men step on one side, and then they get all grime with mire, though the steps be there ; but the ground is good when they are once got in at the gate."

CHAPTER III.

WORLDLY-WISEMAN.

AS Christian took his lone walk he saw one cross the field to meet him, and their hap was to meet just as they did cross the same way. The man's name was Mr. Worldly-wiseman. Hence Mr. Worldly-wiseman thus held some talk with Christian.

Wor.—"How now, good friend ; where dost thou go bent down with such a weight ?"

CHRISTIAN AND WORLDLY-WISEMAN

Chr.—" As big a load, in sooth, as I think a poor wight had in his life! I am bound for yon small gate in front of me: for there, as I am told, I shall be put in a way to be rid of my huge load."

Wor.—" Wilt thou give heed to me, if I tell thee what course to take?"

Chr.—" If what you say be good, I will; for I stand in need of a wise guide."

Wor.—" Who bid thee go this way to be rid of **thy** load?"

Chr.—" A man that I thought was high and great; his name, as my mind serves me, is Evangelist."

Wor.—" There is not a more rough way to be found in the world than is that he hath bade thee take; and that thou shalt find if thou wilt be led by him. Hear me: I have seen more years than thou. Thou art like to meet with, on the way which thou dost go, great griefs, pain, lack of food and clothes, sword, fierce beasts, gloom, and, in a word, death, and what not! And why should a man run such risks, just on the word of a strange guide?"

Chr.—" Why, sir, I think I care not what things I meet with in the way, if so be I can get ease from my pack."

Wor.—" But why wilt thou seek for ease this way, as such dire ills go with it? the more so, hadst thou but borne with me, I could aid thee to get what thou dost wish, free from the risks that thou in this way wilt run."

Chr.—" Pray, sir, make known this boon to me."

Wor.—" Why, in yon town (the town is known as Morality) there dwells a squire whose name is Legality, a man of good name, that has skill to help men off with such loads as thine from their backs. To him, as I said, thou canst go and get help in a trice; and if he should not be at home, he hath a fair young son, whose name is Civility, that can do it as well as his sage sire."

Now was Christian at a stand what to do; but soon he thought, "If this be true which this squire hath said, my best course is to be led by him"; and with that he thus spake more.

Chr.—"Sir, which is the way to this good man's house?"

Wor.—"By that hill you must go, and the first house you come at is his."

So Christian went out of his way to go to Mr. Legality's house for help. But lo, when he was got now hard by the hill, that side of it that was next the path did hang so much, that Christian durst not move on, lest the hill should fall on his head: for which cause there he stood still, and he wot not what to do. But soon there came fierce flames of fire out of the hill, each flash of which made Christian dread he should be burnt. And now he was wroth for the heed he gave to Mr. Worldly-wiseman's words. And with that he saw Evangelist come forth to meet him; and thus did he speak with Christian:

"What dost thou here?" said he. At which words Christian knew not what to say. Then said Evangelist to him, "Art not thou the man that I found in tears back of the walls of the City of Destruction?"

Chr.—"Yes, dear sir, I am the man. I met with a squire, so soon as I had got clear of the Slough of Despond, who made me think that I might, in the town which did face me, find a man that could take off my load."

Evan.—"What said that squire to you?"

Chr.—"He bid me with speed get rid of my load; and said I, 'I am hence bound for yon gate to gain more news how I may get to the place where my load may be cast off.'

So he said that he would show me the best way: 'which way,' said he, 'will take you to a squire's house that hath skill to take off these loads.' So I put faith in him, and set out of that way till I came to this, if so be I might soon get ease from my load."

Then said Evangelist, "Stand still a short time, that I may show thee the words of God."

Then Christian fell down at his feet as dead, and did cry, "Woe is me, for I am lost!" At the sight of which Evangelist caught him by the right hand, and said, "Be not frail, but have faith."

Then Evangelist went on, and said, "Give heed to the things that I shall tell thee of. The man that met thee is one Worldly-wiseman, and he bears a fit name; in part, for that his creed is what the world holds; and in part, for that he loves such faith best, for it saves him from the cross. Now, there are three things in this man's words that thou must be sure and shun—his scheme to turn thee out of the way; his wish to make the cross a shame to thee; and his guile, which did tempt thee to set thy feet in that way that leads to death.

"And for this thou must bear in mind to whom he sent thee, no less than his lack of skill to rid thee of thy load. He to whom thou wast sent for ease, by name Legality, has not the gift to set thee free from thy load. No man, as yet, got rid of his load by him: no, nor till the end of time is like to be. 'By the works of the law none can be made just,' for by the deeds of the law no man that lives can be rid of his load; and as for his son, Civility, though he wears soft looks, he is but a knave, and must fail to help thee. Trust me, there is naught else in all this noise that thou hast heard of this spot but a scheme to lure thee of thy soul's bliss."

Now Christian felt sure fear of death, and burst out in a shrill cry, full of woe, as he did curse the time in which he met with Mr. Worldly-wiseman. Still did he say he was the chief of fools for the heed he gave to him. This done, he spoke to Evangelist in words and sense thus:

Chr.—"Sir, what think you? Is there hope? May I now go back and go up to the small gate? Shall I not be sent back from thence in shame?"

Then said Evangelist to him, "Thy sin is most great, for by it thou hast done two bad deeds: thou hast left the way that is good to tread in wrong paths, yet will the man at the gate let thee pass, for he has *good-will* for men."

Then did Christian make up his mind to go back, and Evangelist, when he did kiss his cheek, gave him a smile, and bid him God speed.

CHAPTER IV.

THE WICKET-GATE.

So Christian went on with haste, nor spake he to a man by the way; nor if a man spoke to him, would he deign him a word; so in course of time Christian got up to the gate. Now at the top of the gate there were writ these words:

"Knock, and it shall ope to you."

Hence he did knock more than once or twice.

At last there came a grave man to the gate, whose name was Goodwill, who sought to know who was there? and whence he came? and what he would have?

Chr.—"Here is a poor vile wight; I come from the City of Destruction, but am bound for Mount Zion, that I may get safe from the wrath to come. I would, for this cause, sir, know if you will let me in."

"I will, with all my heart," said he; and with that he drew back the gate.

So when he was got in, the man of the gate said to him, "Who told him to come to that place?"

Chr.—"Evangelist bid me come here and knock, as I did; and he said that you, sir, would tell me what I must do."

Good.—"But how is it that no one came with you?"

Chr.—"For that none of those who dwelt near me saw their plight as I saw mine."

Good.—"Did one or more of them know that you meant to come here?"

Chr.—"Yes; my wife and bairns saw me at the first, and did call to me to turn round."

Good.—"But did none of them go in quest of you, to urge you to go back?"

Chr.—"Yes, both Obstinate and Pliable; but when they saw that they could not gain their end, Obstinate went back, and did rail the while, but Pliable came with me a short way."

Good.—"But why did he not come through?"

Chr.—"We, in truth, came on side by side till we came to the Slough of Despond, in the which he fell souse. But as he got out on that side next to his own house, he told me I should hold the brave land for him. So he went his way, and I came mine."

Then said Goodwill, "Ah, poor man!"

"In sooth," said Christian. "I have said the truth of

Pliable; but I, too, did turn on one side to go in the way of death, and I was led to this by the base arts of one Mr. Worldly-wiseman."

Good.—" Oh, did he light on you? What! he would have had you seek for ease at the hands of Mr. Legality :

CHRISTIAN AT THE WICKET-GATE.

they are both of them true cheats. But were you led by him?"

Chr.—" Yes, as far as I durst. I went to find out Mr. Legality, till I thought the mount that stands by his house would have come down on my head."

Good.—" That mount has been the death of a host, and will be the death of still more."

Chr.—" Why, in truth, I do not know what hap had come to me there, had not Evangelist by good luck met me once more, while I did muse in the midst of my dumps : but it was God's grace that he came to me twice, for else I could not have got to this place."

Good.—" We shut out none, and take no note of what they have done up to the time they come here: 'they in no wise are cast out': and hence, good Christian, come a wee way with me, and I will teach thee in what way thou must go.   Look right in front of thee ; dost thou see this strait way ?   That is the way thou must go."

" But," said Christian, " are there no turns or bends by which one who has not trod it may lose his way ? "

Good.—" Yes, there are some ways butt down on this ; and they are bent and wide : but thus thou canst judge the right from the wrong, that the first is straight and not broad."

Then Christian strove to gird up his loins, and to set out on his way.   So he with whom he had held speech told him, " That by that he had gone some way from the gate he would come at the house of the Interpreter, at whose door he should knock, and he would show him good things."

CHAPTER V.

THE INTERPRETER'S HOUSE.

THEN he went on till he came to the house of the Interpreter, at which he gave some smart knocks.   At last one came to the door, and did ask who was there ?

"Sir," said Christian, "I am a man that am come from the City of Destruction, and am bound for the Mount Zion ; and I was told by the man that stands at the gate at the head of this way, that if I came here you would show me good things, such as would be a help to one on the road."

Then said the Interpreter, "Come in ; I will show thee that which will be of use to thee." So he told his man to light the lamp, and bid Christian go in his track. Then he had him in a room where none else could come, and bid his man fold back the door, the which when he had done Christian saw the print of one, most grave of look, hung up on the wall, and this was the style of it : It had eyes that did stare at the sky, the best of books in its hand, and the law of truth was writ on its lips ; the world was at its back, it stood as if it did plead with men, and a crown of gold did hang nigh its head.

Then said Christian, " What means this ? "

Inter.—" I have shown thee this print first for this cause, that the man whose print this is, is the sole man whom the Lord of the place where thou dost go hath sent as thy guide through all the twists and turns thou wilt meet with in the way ; hence take good heed to what I have shown thee, and bear well in thy mind what thou hast seen, lest, in thy route, thou meet with some that say they can lead thee right ; but their way goes down to death."

Then he took him by the hand, and led him to a large room on the ground floor that was full of dust ; the which the Interpreter did call for a man to sweep. Then said the Interpreter to a girl that stood by, " Bring hence from yon brook the means to lay this dust."

Then said Christian, " What means this ? "

The Interpreter thus spoke: " This room on the ground floor is the heart of man that has not been made pure by the sweet grace of Christ's Word. The *dust* is the sin that cleaves to him through the Fall, and the lust that hath made foul the whole man. He who at first swept is the Law; but she that brought the means to lay the dust is the Gospel."

I saw too, in my dream, that the Interpreter took him by the hand, and had him in a small room, where sat two youths, each one in his chair. The name of the most grown was Passion, and of the next, Patience: Passion did not seem at rest, but Patience was quite still.

Then I saw that one came to Passion and brought him a bag of rich gifts, and did pour it down at his feet; the which he took up and felt joy in it, while at Patience he gave a laugh of scorn. But I saw but a time, and he had got rid of all, and had naught left but rags.

Then said Christian to the Interpreter, " I would have you make this thing more clear to me."

So he said, " These two lads are signs: Passion of the men of this world, and Patience of the men of that which is to come; for, as here thou dost see, Passion will have all now, this year, that is to say in this world, so are the men of this world; they must have all their good things now; they durst not stay till next year, that is till the next world, for their share of good."

Then said Christian, " Now I see that Patience has the best sense, and that on more grounds than one; for that he stays for the best things, and in like way for that he will have the gain of his when Passion has naught but rags."

Inter.—" Nay, you may add one more, to wit, the joys

INTERPRETER. SHOWS. CHRISTIAN. THE. ROOM. FULL. OF. DUST

of the next world will not wear out, but these are soon gone."

I saw, in like way, that the Interpreter took him once more by the hand, and led him to a choice place, where was built a great house, fine to look at; at the sight of which Christian felt much joy; he saw, too, on the top of it some folk that did walk to and fro, who were clad all in gold.

Then the Interpreter took him, and led him up nigh to the door of the great house; and lo, at the door stood a host of men as did wish to go in, but durst not. There, too, sat a man a short way from the door, at the side of a board, with a book and his desk in front of him, to take the name of him that should come in. More than this, he saw that in the porch stood groups of men, clad in coats of mail, to keep it, who meant to do all the hurt and harm they could to the man that would go in. Now was Christian in a sore maze. At last, when all the men did start back for fear of the men who bore arms, Christian saw a man of a bold face come up to the man that sat there to write, and say, "Set down my name, sir"; the which when he had done, he saw the man draw his sword, and put a casque on his head, and rush to the door on the men who had arms, who laid on him with fierce force; but the man, not at all put out of the way, fell to, and did cut and hack with all his might: so, when he had got and dealt scores of wounds to those that strove to keep him out, he cut his way through them all, and made straight for the great house.

"Now," said Christian, "let me go hence."

"Nay, stay," said the Interpreter, "till I have shown thee some more; and then thou shalt go on thy way."

Just as Christian came up with the cross, his load got loose from his neck, and fell from off his back.

(The Pilgrim's Progress.)

So he took him by the hand once more, and led him to a room dark as pitch, where there sat a man in a steel cage. Now the man to look on was most sad; and he gave sighs as if he would break his heart.

The man said, " I once did seem to be what I was not fair in mine own eyes, and in the eyes of those that knew me. I was once, as I thought, fair for the Celestial City, and went so far as to have joy at the thoughts that I should get there."

Chr.—" Well, but what art thou now ? "

Man.—" I am now a man lost to hope."

Chr.—" But how didst thou get in this state ? "

Man.—" I did sin in face of the light of the World, and the grace of God. I made the Spirit grieve, and he is gone."

Then said Christian, " Is there no hope, but you must be kept in the steel cage of gloom ? "

Man.—" None at all."

Chr.—" But canst thou not now grieve and turn ? "

Man.—" God hath not let me ; his Word gives me no aid to faith ; yea, he hath shut me up in this steel cage ; nor can all the men in the world let me out."

Then said the Interpreter to Christian, " Let this man's wails be dwelt on by thee, and cease not to teach thee how to act."

So he took Christian and led him to a room where one did rise out of bed ; and as he put on his clothes he did shake and quake.

Then said Christian, " Why doth this man thus shake?"

So he spoke and said, " This night as I was in my sleep I dreamt, and lo, the sky grew black as ink, when flame flit from the clouds ; on which I heard a dread noise, that put me in throes of pain. So I did lift up my eyes in my dream, and saw a man sit on a cloud, with a huge host near to him. I heard, then, a voice that said, 'Come forth, ye dead, and meet your Judge!' And with that the rocks rent, the graves did gape, and the dead that were in them came forth. Then I saw the man that sat on the cloud fold back the book and bid the world draw near. I heard it, in like way, told to them that were near the man that sat on the cloud, 'Bind up the tares, and the chaff, and the stalks, and cast them in the lake that burns with fire.' Then said the voice to the same men, 'Put up my wheat in the barn!' and with that I saw a host caught up in the clouds, but I was left stay."

Chr.—" But what was it that made you so quake at this sight ? "

Man.—" Why, I thought that the day of doom had come, and that I was not fit to meet it. But this made me fear most, that some were caught up while I was left."

Then said the Interpreter to Christian, " Hast thou thought well on all these things ? "

Chr.—" Yes ; and they put me in hope and fear."

Inter.—" Well, keep all things so in thy mind that they may be as a goad in thy sides, to prick thee on in the way thou must go."

Then Christian girt up his loins, and thought but of the long road he had to tread.

So I saw that just as Christian came up to the cross, his load
cut loose from his neck, and fell from off his back.—Page 25.

Pilgrim's Progress.

CHAPTER VI.

THE CROSS AND THE CONTRAST.

Now I saw in my dream that the high road had on each side a wall for a fence, and that wall went by the name of Salvation. Up this way, then, did Christian run with his load, till he came to a place where was a high slope, and on that place stood a cross, and a short way from it in the vale, a tomb. So I saw in my dream that just as Christian came up with the cross, his load got loose from his neck, and fell from off his back, and did roll till it came to the mouth of the grave, where it fell in, and I saw it no more.

Then was Christian full glad, and said, with a gay heart, "He hath brought me rest by his grief, and life by his death." Then he stood still for a short time to look with awe, for it was a strange thing to him that the sight of the cross should thus ease him of his load.

I saw then in my dream that he went on thus till he came to a vale, where he saw three men in deep sleep, with gyves on their heels. The name of the one was Simple; the next, Sloth; and the third, Presumption.

Christian went to them, if so be he might rouse them; so he said in a loud voice, "You are like them that sleep on the top of a mast, for the Dead Sea is low down at your feet, a gulf that no plumb line can sound; get up, hence and come on."

With this they gave a glum look at him, and spoke in this sort: Simple said, "I see no cause for fear"; Sloth said, "Yet some more sleep"; and Presumption said,

"Each tub must stand on its own end." And so they lay down to sleep once more, and Christian went on his way.

Yet felt he grief to think that men in that sad plight should so spurn the kind act of him that of his own free will sought to help them. And as he did grieve from this

FORMALIST AND HYPOCRISY COMING INTO THE WAY OVER THE WALL.

cause, he saw two men roll off a wall, on the left hand of the strait way. The name of the one was Formalist, and the name of the next Hypocrisy. So they drew up nigh him, who thus held speech with them:

Chr.—"Sirs, whence came you, and where do you go?"

Form. and Hyp.—" We were born in the land of Vain glory, and are bent for praise to Mount Zion."

Chr.—" Why came you not in at the gate which stands at the head of the way ? "

They said, " That to go to the gate to get in was by all their horde thought too far round."

Chr.—" But will it not be thought a wrong done to the Lord of the town where we are bound, thus to break his law which he hath made known to us ? "

They told him, " That this act of theirs, as it stood for so long a time, would no doubt be thought good in law by a just judge; and more than this," said they, " if we get in the way, what boots it which way we get in ? If we are in, we are in. Thou art but in the way, who, as we see, came in at the gate ; and we too are in the way, that fell from the top of the wall. In what, now, is thy state a whit more good than ours ? "

Chr.—" I walk by the rule of my Lord ; you walk by the rude quirks of your vague whims. At this time you count but as thieves in the sight of the Lord of the way hence I doubt you will not be found true men at the end of the way. By laws and rules you will not get safe, since you came not in by the door. I have, too, a mark on my brow, which you may not have seen, which one of my Lord's most stanch friends put there, in the day that my load fell from off my back. More than this, I will tell you that I then got a roll with a seal on it, to cheer me while I read it, as I go on the way : I was told to give it in at the Celestial Gate, as a sure sign that I, too, should go in at the right time : all which things I doubt you want, and want them for that you came not in at the gate."

CHAPTER VII.

THE HILL DIFFICULTY.

I saw then that they all went on till they came to the foot of the Hill Difficulty, at the end of which was a spring. There were in the same place two ways more than that which came straight from the gate: one bent to the left hand, and the next to the right, at the base of the hill; but the strait way lay right up the hill; and the name of that path up the side of the hill is known as Difficulty. Christian now went to the spring and drank of it to cool his blood and quench his thirst, and then he set forth to go up the hill.

The two with whom he had held speech in like way came to the foot of the hill; but when they saw that the hill was steep and high, and that there were two more ways to go, and as they thought that these two ways might meet in the long run with that up which Christian went, on the rear side of the hill,—hence they made up their minds to go in those ways.

Now the name of one of those ways was Danger, and the name of the next Destruction. So the one took the way which is known as Danger, which led him to a great wood; and he who was with him took straight up the way to Destruction, which led to a wide field full of dark cliffs, where he made a slip, and fell, and rose no more.

I then cast my eyes on Christian, and I saw that from a run he came to a walk, and at last had to climb on his hands and his knees, so steep was the place.

Now half the way *to* the top of the hill was a nook made

Timorous was afraid of wild beasts and ran down the hill.—
Page 29.   *Pilgrim's Progress.*

of trees, fair to look on, made by the Lord of the hill for the good of such as trod that place. There, then, Christian got; there, too, he sat down to rest him.

Thus sought he cheer a while, when he fell to doze, and then went off in a fast sleep.

Now as he slept there came one to him, who woke him and said, "Go to the ant, thou man of sloth; think of her ways, and be wise." And with that Christian did start up, and went on till he came to the top of the hill.

Now when he was got up to the top of the hill, there came two men who ran right up to him so as to push him. The name of the one was Timorous, and of the next Mistrust; to whom Christian said, "Sirs, what doth ail you? You run the wrong way."

Timorous said that they were bound to the City of Zion, and had got up to that hard place; "but," said he, "the more we go on the more risks we meet with; hence did we turn, and mean not to go back."

"Yes," said Mistrust, "for just in front of us lie a brace of wild beasts in the way—that they sleep or wake we know not—and we could not think if we came in their reach but they would at once pull us in bits."

Then Mistrust and Timorous ran down the hill, and Christian went on his way. But as he dwelt on what he heard from the men, the sun went down; and this made him once more think how vain it was for him to have sunk to sleep. Now, he brought to mind the tale that Mistrust and Timorous had told him of how they took fright at the sight of the wild beasts. Then did Christian muse thus: "These beasts range in the night for their prey; and if they should meet with me in the dark, how should I shift them! how should I get free from their fangs? they would tear me to bits." Thus he went on his way. But, while he did mourn his dire hap, he lift up his eyes, and lo, there was a grand house in front of him, the name of which was Beautiful, and it stood just on the side of the high road.

CHAPTER VIII.

THE PALACE BEAUTIFUL.

So I saw in my dream that he made haste and went forth, that, if so be, he might get a place to lodge there. Now ere he had gone far, he saw two wild beasts in the way. (The beasts were made fast, but he saw not the chains.) Then he took fright, and thought to go back; for he thought death of a truth did face him. But when the man at the lodge, whose name is Watchful, saw that Christian made a halt, he did cry to him and say, "Is thy strength so small? Fear not the wild beasts, for they are in chains, and are put there for test of faith where it is, and to make known those that have none: keep in the midst of the path, and no hurt shall come to thee."

Then did he clap his hands, and went on till he came and stood in front of the gate where the Porter was. Then said Christian to the Porter, "Sir, what house is this? and may I lodge here this night?" The Porter said, "This house was built by the Lord of the hill, and he built it to aid and guard such as speed this way." The Porter, in like way, sought to know whence he was; and to what place he was bound?

Chr.—"I am come from the City of Destruction; and

This is Mistrust, whom Christian met going the wrong way.—
Page 29.   *Pilgrim's Progress.*

am on my way to Mount Zion; but as the sun is now set, I wish, if I may, to lodge here this night."

Por.—"But how doth it hap that you come so late? The sun is set."

Chr.—"I had been here ere this, but that, mean man that I am, I slept in the nook that stands on the side of the hill."

Por.—"Well, I will call out one of the maids of this place, who will, if she likes your talk, bring you in to the rest of the folk, as such are the rules of the house."

So Watchful rang a bell, at the sound of which came out at the door of the house a grave and fair maid, whose name was Discretion, who would know why she had got a call.

The Porter said, "This man is in the way from the City of Destruction to Mount Zion, but as he doth tire, and as night came on, he sought to know if he might lodge here for the night: so I told him I would call for thee, who, when thou dost speak with him, may do as seems to thee good, and act up to the law of the house."

Then she would know whence he was, and to what place he was bound, and his name. So he said, "It is Christian." So a smile sat on her lips, but the tears stood in her eyes; and, when she gave a short pause, she said, "I will call forth two or three more of those who dwell here." So she ran to the door, and did call out Prudence, Piety, and Charity; and when she had held more speech with him, he was brought in, and made known to all who dwelt in the house, some of whom met him at the porch, and said, "Come in, thou whom the Lord doth bless; this house was built by the Lord of the hill, to give good cheer to such who, like you, grow faint by the way." Then he bent his head, and went in with them to the house. So when he was come in and set down, they gave him to drink, and then they thought that till the last meal was brought up, some of them should have some wise talk with Christian, so as to make good use of time.

CHRISTIAN IS QUESTIONED BY DISCRETION.

Pi.—"Come, good Christian, since we have shown such love for you as to make you our guest this night, let us, if so be we may each get good by it, talk with you of all things that you have met with on your way."

This is Formalist, whom Christian saw roll from the top of
a wall, as if to go to Zion.—Page 53.   *Pilgrim's Progress.*

Chr.—"With a right good will; and I am glad your mind is so well bent."

Pi.—"How was it that you came out of your land in this way?"

Chr.—"It was as God would have it; for when I was full of the fears of doom, I did not know where to go; but by chance there came a man then to me, whilst I shook and wept, whose name is Evangelist, and he told me how to reach the small gate, which else I should not have found, and so set me in the way that hath led me straight to this house."

Pi.—"But did you not come by the house of the Interpreter?"

Chr.—"Yes, and did see such things there, the thoughts of which will stick by me as long as I live; in chief, three things; to wit, how Christ, in spite of the Foe of Man, keeps up his work of grace in the heart; how the man, through sin, had got quite out of hopes of God's ruth; and, in like way, the dream of him that thought in his sleep the day of doom was come."

Pi.—"And what saw you else in the way?"

Chr.—"Saw! Why, I went but a wee way and I saw One, as I thought in my mind, hang and bleed on a tree; and the sheer sight of him made my load fall off my back; for I did groan through the great weight, but then it fell down from off me."

Pi.—"But you saw more than this, did you not?"

Chr.—"The things that I have told you were the best; yet some more things I saw, as, first of all, I saw three men, Simple, Sloth, and Presumption, lie in sleep, not far out of the way as I came, with gyves on their heels; but do you think I could rouse them? I saw, in like way, Formalist and Hypocrisy come and roll from the top of a wall, to go, as they fain would have me think, to Zion ; but they were lost in a trice, just as I did tell them ; but they would not heed my words."

Pr.—" Do you think at times of the land from whence you came ? "

Chr.—" Yes, but with much shame and hate."

Pr.—" Do you not yet bear hence with you some of the things that you well knew there ? "

Chr.—" Yes, but much in strife with my will ; the more so the crass thoughts of my heart, with which all the folk of my land, as well as I, would find joy ; but now all those things are my grief, and might I but choose mine own things, I would choose not to think of those things more ; but when I would do that which is best, that which is worst is with me."

Pr.—" And what is it that makes you so long to go to Mount Zion ? "

Chr.—" Why, there I hope to see Him live that did hang dead on the cross ; and there I hope to be rid of all those things that to this day are in me and do vex me : there they say there is no death ; and there I shall dwell with such folk as I like best."

Then said Charity to Christian, " Have you bairns, and have you a wife ? "

Chr.—" I have a wife and four small bairns."

Char.—" And why did you not bring them on with you?"

Then Christian wept and said, " Oh, fain would I have done it ! but they were all of them loath to let me leave them."

Char.—"But you should have sought to show them the risks they ran when they held back."

Hypocrisy would fain nave Christian think he was on the way
to Zion.—Page 34.   *Pilgrim's Prog 's.*

Chr.—" So I did; and told them, too, that God had shown to me how that our town would come to wrack; but they thought I did but mock, and they put no faith in what I said."

Char.—" But what could they say to show cause why they came not ? "

CHRISTIAN TELLS CHARITY AND HER SISTERS ABOUT HIS FAMILY.

Chr.—" Why, my wife was loath to lose this world; and my bairns were bent on the rash joys of youth: so, what by this thing, and what by that thing, they left me to roam in this lone way."

Char.—" But did you not with your vain life damp all

that you by words made use of as force to bring them off
with you?"

Chr.—"In sooth, I must not say aught for my life, as I
know full well what blurs there are in it. I know, too,
that a man by his deeds may soon set at naught what by
sound speech and wit of words he doth strive to fix on
some for their good. Yet this I can say, I took heed not
to give them cause, by a false act, to shirk the step I took,
and not set out with me. Yea, for this sole thing they
would tell me I was too nice; and that I would not touch
of things in which they saw no guile."

Char.—"In truth, Cain did hate him who came of the
same blood, for that his works were bad, and Abel's not
so; and if thy wife and bairns have thought ill of thee for
this, they show by it that they are foes to good; and thou
hast set free thy soul from their blood."

Now I saw in my dream that thus they sat and spoke
each to each till the meal was laid on the board; and all
their talk while they ate was of the Lord of the hill; as,
in sooth, of what he had done, and why it was he did what
he did, and why he had built that house.

They, in like way, gave prompt proof of what they said,
and that was, he had stript him of his rich robes, that he
might do this for the poor; and that they heard him say,
with stern stress, that he would not dwell in the Mount of
Zion in a lone way. They said, too, that he made a host
of poor ones kings, though by the law of their birth they
were born to live on bare alms, and their first state had
been low and bad.

Thus they spoke, this one to that one, till late at night;
and when they had put them in the Lord's care they went
to rest.

Then he set forth: but Discretion, Piety, Charity, and Prudence would go with him down to the foot of the hill.

(The Pilgrim's Progress.)

The next day they took him and had him in the place in which arms were kept, where he was shown all sorts of things which their Lord had put there for such as he, as sword, shield, casque, plate for breast, *All-prayer*, and shoes that would not wear out. And there was here as much of this as would fit out a host of men to serve the Lord.

In like way did they show him some of the means with which some of his friends had done things that strike one with awe. He was shown the jaw-bone of the ass with which Samson did such great feats. More than this, he was shown the sling and stone with which David slew Goliath of Gath. But more things still were shown to him, in all of which Christian felt much joy. This done, they went to their rest once more.

Then I saw in my dream that on the morn he got up to go forth, but they fain would have him stay till the next day; "and then," said they, "we will, if the day be clear, show you the Delectable Mountains, which," they said, "would yet the more add to his bliss, for that they were yet more nigh the port than the place where at that time he was." So he thought it well to stay.

When the morn was up, they had him to the top of the house, and bid him look south; so he did, and lo, a long way off, he saw a fair land, full of high hills, clad with woods, vine grounds, fruits of all sorts, plants as well, with springs and founts, most bright to look on. They said it was Immanuel's Land; "and it is as free," said they, "as this hill is to and for all that are in the way. And when thou dost come there from thence," said they, "thou canst see to the gate of the Celestial City, as those who watch their flocks and live there will show thee."

Now he thought it was due time to set forth, and they were glad that he should. "But first," said they, "let us go once more to where the arms are kept." So they did. And when he came there they clad him in coat of mail, which was of proof, from head to foot, lest he should chance meet with foes in the way.

He then, in this gear, came out with his friends to the gate, and there he would know of the Porter "if he saw one pass by?"

Then the Porter said "Yes."

Chr.—"Pray did you know him?"

Por.—"I did ask his name, and he told me it was Faithful."

"Oh," said Christian, "I know him: he is from the same town, and lives nigh to where I dwell: he comes from the place where I was born. How far do you think he may be on the road?"

Por.—"He has got by this time more than to the foot of the hill."

Then he set forth: but Discretion, Piety, Charity, and Prudence would go with him down to the foot of the hill. Then said Christian, "As it was *hard* to come up, so, so far as I can see, it is a *risk* to go down." "Yes," said Prudence, "so it is; for it is a hard thing for a man to go down in the Vale of Humiliation, as thou art now, and to catch no slip by the way; hence," said they, "we are come out to see thee safe down the hill." So he strove to go down, but with great heed; yet he caught a slip or two.

Then I saw in my dream that these good friends, when Christian was gone down to the foot of the hill, gave him a loaf of bread, a flask of wine, and a bunch of dry grapes; and then he went on his way.

CHAPTER IX.

APOLLYON.

BUT now, in this Vale of Humiliation, poor Christian was hard put to it ; for he had gone but a short way, when he saw a foul fiend come through the field to meet him : his name is Apollyon.

So he went on, and Apollyon met him. Now the ghoul did shock one's eyes to look on : he was clad with scales like a fish ; he had wings like a huge bat, feet like a bear, and out of his throat came fire and smoke, and his mouth was as the mouth of the king of beasts. When he came up to Christian he gave him a look of scorn, and thus sought to sift him.

Apol.—" Whence came you ? and to what place are you bound ? "

Chr.—" I am come from the City of Destruction, which is the place of all ill, and am on my way to Mount Zion."

Apol.—" By this I know thou art one of my serfs ; for all that land is mine ; and I am the prince and god of it." How is it, then, that thou hast run off from thy king ? Were it not that I hope thou wilt serve me yet more, I would strike thee now at one blow to the ground."

Chr.—" I was born, in sooth, in your realm, but to serve thee was hard, and your pay such as a man could not live on ; ' for the meed of sin is death ': for this cause, when I was come to years, I did, as some who think do, look out if so be I might mend my state. I have let my help to some one else ; and to no less than the King of Kings."

Apol.—"Think yet, while thou art in cool blood, what thou art like to meet with in the way that thou dost go. Thou art not blind that for the most part those who serve him come to an ill end, for that they spurn my laws and walk not in my paths. What a host of them have been put to deaths of shame! And still thou dost count that to serve him is best; when, in sooth, he has not yet come from the place where he is, to save one that stood by his cause, out of my hands."

Chr.—"He does not seek so soon to save them, so as to try their love, and find if they will cleave to him to the end; and as for the ill end thou dost say they come to, that tells for their good: for to be set free now they do not much look for it; for they stay for their meed; and they shall have it when their Prince comes in the might of the bright hosts that wait on him."

Apol.—"Thou hast erst been false in thy turns to serve him; and how dost thou think to get pay of him?"

Chr.—"All this is true; but the Prince whom I serve and love is sure to show ruth. But, let me say, these faults held hold of me in thy land; for there I did suck them in, and they have made me groan and grieve for them; whence I have got the grace of my Prince."

Then Apollyon broke out in a sore rage, and said, "I am a foe to this Prince: I hate him, his laws, and they who serve him. I am come out with the view to make thee yield."

Chr.—"Apollyon, take heed what you do; for I am on the King's high road, the way of grace; for which cause mind how you act."

Then did Christian draw; for he saw it was time for him to stir; and Apollyon as fast made at him, and threw darts as thick as hail, by the which, in spite of all that Christian could do to shift it, Apollyon hit him in his head, his hand, and foot. This made Christian give some back : Apollyon then went to his work with heart, and Christian once more took heart, and met his foe as well as he could.

Then Apollyon, as he saw his time had come, made up close to Christian, and as he strove to throw him gave him a dread fall ; and with that Christian's sword flew out of his hand. Then said Apollyon, " I am sure of thee now ! " and with that he did nigh press him to death ; so that Christian had slight hope of life. But, as God would have it, while Apollyon dealt his last blow, by that means to make a full end of this good man, Christian at once put out his hand for his sword, caught it, and said, " When I fall, I shall then rise "; and with that gave him a fierce thrust, which made him give back as one that had got his death wound. Christian saw that, and made at him once more, while he said, " Nay, in all these things we more than gain the prize through him that loves us "; and with that Apollyon spread forth his foul wings and sped him off, that Christian saw no more of him.

So when the fight came to a close, Christian said, " I will here give thanks to him that hath kept me out of the mouth of the chief of beasts, to him that did help me in the strife with Apollyon."

Then there came to him a hand with some of the leaves of the " tree of life," the which Christian took and laid them on the wounds that he had got in the strife, and was made whole at once.

CHAPTER X.

THE VALLEY OF THE SHADOW OF DEATH.

Now at the end of this vale was one more, known as the Vale of the Shade of Death, and Christian must needs go through it, for this cause, that the way to the Celestial City lay through the midst of it.

I saw then in my dream, so far as the bounds of the vale, there was on the right hand a most deep ditch; that ditch is it to which the blind have led the blind in each age, and have both there lost their lives.

Once more, lo, on the left hand there was a fell quag, in the which, strange to say, if a good man falls he finds no ground for his foot to stand on.

The path was here quite strait, and hence good Christian was the more put to it; for when he sought in the dark to shun the ditch on the one hand, he was prone to tip on one side souse in the mire on the next.

Nigh the midst of the vale I saw the mouth of hell to be, and it stood, too, hard by the side of the way. And at times the flame and smoke would come out so thick and with such force, that he had to put up his sword and seize more fit arms, known as *All-prayer;* so I heard him cry, "O Lord, I pray thee save my soul!"

Thus he went on a great while; and as he came to a place where he thought he heard a band of fiends come forth to meet him, he stopt, and did muse what he had best to do. He brought to mind how he had of late held his foes at bay, and that the risk to go back might be much more than to go on. So he made up his mind to go on:

yet the fiends did seem to come near and more near. But when they were come just at him he did cry with a loud voice, " I will walk in the strength of the Lord God ": so they gave back, and came on no more.

When Christian had trod on in this lorn state some length of time, he thought he heard the voice of a man, as if in front of him, say thus: " Though I walk through the vale of the shade of death I will fear no ill : for Thou art with me."

Then was he glad for that he learnt from thence that some who fear God were in this vale as well as he ; that God was with them, though in that dark and dire state. So he went on. And by and by the day broke. Then said Christian, " He doth turn the shade of death to morn."

Now as morn had come, he gave a look back to see by the light of the day what risks he had gone through in the dark. So he had a more clear view of the ditch that was on the one hand, and the quag that was on the next ; in like way he saw how strait the way was which lay twixt them both. And just at this time the sun rose ; and this was one more boon to Christian : for, from the place where he now stood as far as to the end of the vale, the way was all through set so full of snares, traps, gins, and nets, here ; and so full of pits, falls, deep holes, and slopes, down there ; that had it now been dark, as it was when he came the first part of the way, had he had five times ten score souls, they had for this cause been cast off. But, as I said just now, the sun did rise.

In this light hence he came to the end of the vale.

CHAPTER XI.

CHRISTIAN AND FAITHFUL.

Now as Christian went on his way he came to a small height, which was cast up so that those who came that way might see in front of them. Up there, then, Christian went: and, with a glance, saw Faithful some way on the road.

At this Christian set out with all his strength, and soon got up with Faithful, and did, in sooth, leave him lag, so that the last was first. Then did Christian wear a proud smile, for that he had got the start of his friend: but as he did not take good heed to his feet, he soon struck some tuft and fell, and could not rise till Faithful came up to help him.

Then I saw in my dream, they went on with good will side by side, and had sweet talk of all things that they had met with on their way: and thus Christian first spoke:

"My most dear friend Faithful, I am glad I have come up with you; and that God hath so made us of one mind that we can walk as friends in this so fair a path. Tell me now what you have met with in the way as you came: for I know you have met with some things, or else it may be writ for a strange pass."

Fai.—"I got clear of the slough that I see you fell in, and came up to the gate free from that risk. When I came to the foot of the hill known as Difficulty, I met with an old man, who would know what I was, and to what place I was bound? Then said the old man, 'Thou dost look like a frank soul: wilt thou stay and dwell with me

for the pay that I shall give thee?' Then I did ask his name, and where he dwelt? He said, 'His name was Adam the First, and he dwelt in the Town of Deceit.' He told me, 'That his work was fraught with joys, and his pay, that I should be his heir at last.' I then would know what kin he had? He said, 'He had but three maids, "the Lust of the flesh, the Lust of the eyes, and the Pride of life," and that I should wive with one of them, if I would."

Chr.—"Well, and what close came the old man and you to at last?"

Fai.—"Why, at first I would lief go with the man, for I thought he spake full fair; but when I gave a look in his brow, as I spoke with him, I saw there writ, 'Put off the old man with his deeds.' Then it came red hot to my mind, that spite of all he said, and his smooth ways, when he got me home to his house he would sell me for a slave. So I went off from him: but just as I set round to go thence, I felt him take hold of my flesh, and give me such a dread twitch back, that I thought he did pull part of me with him. So I went on my way up the hill.

"Now, when I had got nigh half way up, I gave a look back, and saw one move on in my steps, swift as the wind; so he came up with me just by the place where the bench stands. So soon as the man came up with me, it was but a word and a blow, for down he flung me, and laid me for dead. But, when I got free from the shock, I would know why it was he dealt with me so? He said, 'For that I did in my heart cleave to Adam the First': and with that he struck me one more fierce blow on the breast, and beat me down on the back. He had, no doubt, made an end of me, but that one came by and bid him stay his hand."

This is Discontent, who would fain have Christian go back
with him once more.—Page 47.   *Pilgrim's Progress.*

Chr.—"Who was that that bid him stay his hand?"

Fai.—"I did not know him at first, but as he went by I saw the holes in his hands and in his side: then I felt sure that he was our Lord. So I went up the hill."

Chr.—"That man that came up with you was Moses. He spares not, nor knows he how to show grace to those that break his law. But did you not see the house that stood there on the top of the hill, on the side of which Moses met you?"

Fai.—"Yes, and the wild beasts, too, ere I came at it: but, as I had so much of the day to spend, I came by the man at the lodge, and then down the hill."

Chr.—"But, pray tell me, did you meet with no one in the Vale of Humility?"

Fai.—"Yes, I met with one Discontent, who would fain have me to go back once more with him: his cause was, for that the vale did not bear a good name."

Chr.—"Met you with naught else in that vale?"

Fai.—"Yes, I met with Shame: but of all men that I met with in my way, he, I think, bears the wrong name."

Chr.—"Why, what did he say to you?"

Fai.—"What! Why, he did flout at faith. He said it was a poor, low, mean thing for a man to mind faith; he said that a soul that shrinks from sin is not fit for a man. He said, too, that but few of the great, rich, or wise held my views; nor did those till they were led to be fools, and to be of a free mind to run the loss of all for none else knows what. More than this, he said such were of a base and low caste, and knew naught of those things which are the boast of the wise. Yea, he did hold me to it that it was a shame to ask grace of folk for slight faults, or to give back that which I did take. He said, too, that faith made a man grow strange to the great, and made him own and prize the base : ' and is not this,' said he, ' a shame ? ' "

Chr.—" And what did you say to him ? "

Fai.—" Say ! I could not tell what to say at first. Yea, he put me so to it that my blood came up in my face ; aye, this Shame did fetch it up, and had, too, beat me quite off.

FAITHFUL RESISTS SHAME.

But at last I thought that that which men prize was base in the sight of God. Hence, thought I, what God says is best, *is* best, though all the men in the world are foes to it. As, then, God likes his faith ; as God likes a soul that shrinks from sin ; and as they are most wise who wear the guise of fools to gain a crown : and that the poor man that loves Christ is more rich than the man that sways a world, that hates him; Shame, go thy way, thou art a foe to my soul's weal. But, in sooth, this Shame was a bold knave; I could scarce shake him out of my way: but at last I told him it was but in vain to strive with me from that time forth. And when I shook him off, then I sang—

> " The tests that those men meet, with all men else
>   That bow their wills to the high call of God,
>   Are great; and well, I wist, do suit the flesh,
>   And come, and come, and come e'en yet once more;
>   That now, or some time else, we by them may
>   Be held in thrall, flung down, and cast sheer off:
>   O, let those in the way, let all such, then,
>   Be sharp, and quick, and quit them like true men."

Chr.—" I am glad, my friend, that thou didst strive with this knave in so brave a way; for he is so bold as to trace our steps in the streets, and to try to put us to shame in the sight of all men; that is, to make us feel shame in that which is good."

Fai.—" I think we must cry to Him for help in our frays with Shame, that would have us ' Stand up for truth on the earth.' "

Chr.—" You say true: but did you meet none else in that vale ? "

Fai.—" No, not I; for I had the sun with me all the rest of the way through that, as well as through the Vale of the Shade of Death."

Chr.—" It was well for you; I am sure it did fare far worse with me. I thought I should have lost my life there more than once: but at last day broke, and the sun rose, and I went through that which was to the front of me with far more ease and peace."

CHAPTER XII.

TALKATIVE.

MORE than this, I saw in my dream, that as they went on, Faithful saw a man whose name is Talkative, walk some way off by the side of them : for in this place there was full room for them all to walk. To this man Faithful spoke in such wise :

"Friend, to what place dost thou go? dost thou go to the blest land?"

Talk.—"I am bound to that same place."

Fai.—"Come on then, and let us go side by side, and let us spend our time well, by wise speech that tends to use."

Talk.—"To talk of things that are good, I like much, with you or with some one else. For, to speak the truth, there are but few that care thus to spend their time, as they are on their way."

Fai.—"That is, in sooth, a thing to mourn; for what thing so meet for the use of the tongue and mouth of men on earth, as are the things of the great God on high?"

Talk.—"I like you right well, for what you say is full of force; and, I will add, what thing doth so please or what brings such a boon as to talk of the things of God?"

Fai.—"That is true; but to gain good by such things in our talk, should be that which we seek."

Talk.—"That is it that I said; for to talk of such things is of great use : for by this means a man may get to know a fair share of things; as how vain are the things of earth; and how good are the things that fail not. Then,

Faithful saw a man whose name is Talkative, who said, "Friend,
to what place dost thou go? dost thou go to the blest land?"—
Page 50.   *Pilgrim's Progress.*

by this, a man may learn by talk what it is to mourn for sin, to have faith, to pray, to bear grief, or the like. By this, too, a man may learn what it is that soothes, and what are the high hopes set forth in the Word of the Grace of God; to his own peace."

"Well, then," said Faithful, "what is that one thing that we shall at this time found our speech on?"

Talk.—"What you will: I will talk of things not of earth, or of things of earth; things of life, or things of grace; things pure, or things of the world; so that we but gain good by it."

Now did Faithful think this strange; so he came up to Christian, and said to him in a soft voice, "What a brave friend have we got! Of a truth, this man will do well in the way."

At this Christian gave a meek smile, and said, "This man, whom you so take to, will cheat with this tongue of his a score of them that know him not."

Fai.—"Do you know him then?"

Chr.—"Know him! Yes; his name is Talkative; he dwells in our town. I wist not how you should be strange to him."

Fai.—"Well, he seems to be a man of good looks."

Chr.—"That is, to them that know him not through and through: for he is best out of doors; near home his looks are as bad as you could find."

Fai.—"But I fain think you do but jest, as I saw you smile."

Chr.—"God grant not that I should jest in this case, or that I should speak false of one. I will let you see him in a clear light. This man cares not with whom he picks up, or how he talks: as he talks now with you, so will he talk

when he is on the bench, with ale by his side; and the
more drink he has in his crown, the more of these things
he hath in his mouth."

Fai.—"Say you so? then am I wrong in my thoughts
of this man."

Chr.—"Wrong! You may be sure of it. He talks of
what it is to pray; to mourn for sin; of faith, and of the
new birth; but he knows but how to talk of them. I have
been in his home, and have seen him both in and out of
doors, and I know what I say of him is the truth. His
house is as void of the fear of God as the white of an egg
is of taste. They pray not there, nor is there a sign of
grief for sin: yea, the brute, in his kind, serves God more
than he."

Fai.—"Well, my friend, I am bound to trust you; not
for that you say you know him, but in like way, for that,
like one who has the mind of Christ, you judge of men."

Chr.—"Had I known him no more than you I might, it
may be, have thought of him as at the first you did; but
all these things, yea, and much more as bad, which I do
bring to mind, I can prove him to have the guilt of."

Fai.—"Well, I see that *to say* and *to do* are two things;
and by and by I shall take more note of this."

Cha.—"They are two things, in sooth, and are no more
like than are the soul and flesh; for, as the flesh void of
the soul is but a dead lump: so to *say*, if it stand loose, is
but a dead lump too. This Talkative does not know. He
thinks that to *hear* and to *say* will make a good man, and
thus he cheats his own soul. To hear is but to sow the
seed; to talk is not full proof that fruit is deep in the
heart and life; and let us feel sure that at the day of doom
men shall reap just as they have sown. It will not be said

then, 'Did you have faith?' but 'Did you *do* or *talk?*' when they shall have their due meed."

Fai.—"Well, I was not so fond to be with him at first, but am as sick of him now. What shall we do to be rid of him?"

Chr.—"Be led by me, and do as I bid you, and you shall find that he will soon be sick of you, too, save God shall touch his heart and turn it."

Fai.—"What would you have me to do?"

Chr.—"Why, go to him, and take up some grave theme on the *might* of faith."

Then Faithful gave a step forth once more, and said to Talkative, "Come, what cheer? how is it now?"

Talk.—"Thank you, well; I thought we should have had a great deal of talk by this time."

Fai.—"Well, if you will, we will fall to it now; and since you left it with me to state the theme, let it be this: How doth the grace of God that saves, show forth signs when it is in the heart of man?"

Talk.—"I see, then, that our talk must be of the *might* of things. Well, it is a right good theme, and I shall try to speak on it; and take what I say in brief, thus: First, where the grace of God is in the heart it makes one cry out on sin. In the next place——"

Fai.—"Nay, hold; let us dwell on one at once: I think you should say in lieu of this, it shows by the way in which the soul loathes its sin. A man may cry out on sin to aid his own ends, but he fails to loathe it, save God makes him do so. Some cry out on sin, just as the dame doth cry out on her child in her lap, when she calls it bad girl, and then falls to hug and kiss it."

Talk.—"You lie at the catch, I see."

Fai.—" No, not I; I but try to set things right. But what is the next thing by which you would prove to make known the work of grace in the heart?"

Talk.—" To know much of the deep things of God."

Fai.—" This sign should have been first; but, first or last, it too is false: for to know, and know well, the deep things in God's Word, may still be, and yet no work of grace in the soul. Yea, if a man know all things he may yet be naught; and so, for this cause, be no child of God. When Christ said, 'Do you know all these things?' and those who heard him said, 'Yes'; he did add, 'Blest are ye if ye do them.' He doth not lay the grace in that one *knows*, but in that one *does* them."

Talk.—" You lie at the catch, once more: this is not for good."

Fai.—" Well, if you please, give one more sign how this work of grace doth show where it is."

Talk.—" Not I, for I see we shall not be of one mind."

Fai.—" Well, if you will not, will you give me leave to do it?"

Talk.—" You may do just as you like."

Fai. " A work of grace in the soul doth show quite clear to him that hath it or to those that stand by. To him that hath it, thus: it gives him a deep sense of sin, of the ill that dwells in him. This sight and sense of things work in him grief and shame for sin; he finds, too, brought to view the Saviour of the world, and he feels he must close with him for life; at the which he finds he craves and thirsts for a pure life, pure at heart, pure with his kin, and pure in speech in the world: which in the broad sense doth teach him in his heart to hate his sin, to spurn it from his home, and to shed his light in the world; not by mere talk, as a false knave, or one with a glib tongue, may do, but by the force of faith and love to the might of the Word. And now, sir, as to these brief thoughts on the work of grace, if you have aught to say, say on; if not, then give me leave to ask one thing more of you."

Talk.—"Nay, my part is not now to say aught, but to hear; let me hence hear what you have got to speak."

Fai. "It is this: do you in your heart feel this first part of what I said of it? and doth your life and walk bear proof of the same?"

Then Talkative at first did blush, but when he got through this phase, thus he said: "You come now to what one feels in his heart, to the soul, and God. But I pray, will you tell me why you ask me such things?"

Fai.—"For that I saw you prone to talk, and for that I knew not that you had aught else but vague views. More than this, to tell you all the truth, I have heard of you that you are a man whose faith lies in talk, and that what you do gives the lie to what you say."

Talk.—"Since you are so quick to take up tales, and to judge in so rash a way as you do, I would lief think that you are some cross or dull mope of a man, not fit to hold talk with; and so, I take my leave."

Then came up Christian, and said to his friend, "I told you how it would hap; your words and his lusts could not suit. He thought it best to leave you, than change his life."

Fai.—"But I am glad we had this brief talk; it may hap that he will think of it some time."

Chr.—"You did well to talk so plain to him as you did; there is not much of this straight course with men in these days. I wish that all men would deal with such as you have done: then should they have to change their ways, or the guild of saints would be too hot for them."

Thus they went on and told of what they had seen by the way, and so made that way light which would, were not this the case, no doubt have been slow to them; for now they went through a wild.

CHAPTER XIII.

VANITY FAIR.

Now when they were got all but quite out of this wild, Faithful by chance cast his eye back, and saw one come in his wake, and he knew him. "Oh!" said Faithful to his friend, "who comes yon?"

Then Christian did look, and said, "It is my good friend Evangelist." "Ay, and my good friend, too," said Faithful, "for it was he that set me the way to the gate."

Then said Evangelist, "How did it fare with you, my friends, since the time we last did part? what have you met with, and what has been your life?"

Then Christian and Faithful told him of all things that did hap to them in the way; and how, and with what toil, they had got to that place.

"Right glad am I," said Evangelist, "not that you met with straits, but that you have come safe through them, and for that you have, in spite of some faults, kept in the way to this day. The crown is in sight of you, and it is one that will not rust; 'so run that you may gain it.' You are not yet out of the range of the foul fiend: let the joy of the Lord be not lost sight of, and have a firm faith in things not seen."

Then did Christian thank him for his sage words, but told him at the same time, that they would have him speak more to them for their help the rest of the way. So Evangelist spoke thus:

"My sons, you have heard in the truth of God's Word, that you must pass through sharp straits to reach the realm of bliss; for now as you see you are just out of this wild, and hence you will ere long come to a town that you will by and by see in front of you; and in that town you will be set round with foes, who will strain hard but they will kill you: and be you sure that one or both of you must seal the faith, which you hold, with blood. But when you are come to the town, and shall find what I have said come to pass, then think of your friend, and quit you both like men."

Then I saw in my dream that, when they were got out of the wild, they soon saw a town in front of them; the name of that town is Vanity; and at the town there is a fair kept, known as Vanity Fair; at this fair are all such goods sold as lands, trades, realms, lusts, and gay things of all sorts, as lives, blood, souls, gold, pearls, stones of great worth, and what not.

Now, as I said, the way to the Celestial City lies just through this town where this huge fair is kept: and he that will go there, and yet not go through this town, "must needs go out of the world." The Lord of Lords, when here, went through this town to his own realm, and that, too, on a day when a fair was held: yea, and as I think, it was Beelzebub, the chief lord of this fair, that sought of him to buy of his vain wares. But he had no mind to the goods, and hence left the town, nor did he lay out so much as a mite on these wares.

Now these folk, as I said, must needs go through this fair. Well, so they did; but lo, just as they got to the fair, all the crowd in the fair rose up, and the town, too, as it were, and made much noise and stir for that they came there; they, of course, spoke the tongue of Canaan; but they that kept the fair were the men of this world; so that, from end to end of the fair, they did seem strange each to each. But that which made the crowd most laugh was, that these men set quite light by all their wares: they did not care so much as to look on them; and, if they sought for them to buy, they would stop their ears, and cry, "Turn off mine eyes, lest they see vain things," and look up, to show that their trade and wares were in the skies.

At last things came to a sad pass, which led to great stir in the fair, so that all was noise and din, and law was set at naught. Now was word soon brought to the great one of the fair, who at once came down, and sent some of his best friends to sift those men by whom the fair was put in such a state. So the men were brought in their sight. But they that were sent to sift them did not think them to be aught than fools and mad, or else such as came to put all things out of gear in the fair. Hence they took them and beat them, and made them grime with dirt, and then put them in the cage, that they might be made a foul sight to all the men of the fair. But as the men bore up well, and gave good words for bad, some men in the fair, that were more just than the rest, sought to check and chide the base sort for the vile acts done by them to the men. One said, "That for aught they could see, the men were mild, and of sound mind, and sought to do harm to no one: and that there were some, that did trade in their fair, that ought far more to be put in the

cage, than the men to whom they had done such ill."
Thus, as soon as hot words did pass on both sides, they
fell to some blows, and did harm each to each. Then
were these two poor men brought up once more, when a
charge was made that it was they who had got up the row
that had been made at the fair. But Christian and Faithful
bore the shame and the slur that was cast on them in so
calm and meek a way that it won to their side some of the
men of the fair. This put one part of the crowd in a still
more fierce rage, so that they were bent on the death of
these two men.

Then were they sent back to the cage once more, till it
was told what should be done with them. So they put
them in, and made their feet fast in the stocks.

Here, then, they once more brought to mind what they
had heard from their true friend Evangelist, and were the
more strong in their way and woes by what he told them
would fall out to them. They, too, now sought to cheer
the heart of each, that whose lot it was to die that he
should have the best of it : hence each man did wish in
the depth of his soul that he might have the crown.

Then in due time they brought them forth to court, so
that they might meet their doom. The name of the judge
was Lord Hate-good ; their plaint was "that they had made
broils and feuds in the town, and had won some to their
own most vile views, in scorn of the law of their prince."

Then Faithful said "that he did but spurn that which
had set up in face of Him that is the Most High. And,"
said he, "as for broils, I make none, as I am a man of
peace ; those that were won to us were won by their view
of our truth and pure lives. and they are but gone from the
worst to the best."

Then Superstition said: "My lord, I know not much of this man; but he is a most vile knave."—Page 61. *Pilgrim's Progress.*

Then was it made known that they that had aught to say for their lord the king, to prove the guilt of him at the bar, should at once come forth and give in their proof. So there came in three men, to wit, Envy, Superstition, and Pickthank. Then stood forth Envy and said in this strain: "My lord, this man, in spite of his fair name, is one of the most vile men in our land. He does all that he can to fill all men with some of his wild views, which tend to the bane of our realm, and which he for the most part calls 'grounds of faith and a pure life.' And in chief I heard him once say that the faith of Christ and the laws of our town of Vanity could not be at one, as they were foes each to each."

Then did they call Superstition, and sware him: so he said: "My lord, I know not much of this man, nor do I care to know more of him; but he is a most vile knave; I heard him say that our faith was naught, and such by which no man could please God. Which words of his, my lord, you quite well know what they mean, to wit, that we still work in vain, are yet in our sins, and at last shall be lost. And this is that which I have to say."

Then was Pickthank sworn, and bid say what he knew in the cause of their lord the king to the hurt of the rogue at the bar.

Pick.—"My lord, and you great folk all, this wight I have known of a long time, and have heard him speak things that ought not to be said; for he did rail on our great prince, Beelzebub, and spoke ill of his firm friends; and he hath said, too, that if all men were of his mind, if so be there is not one of these great men should from that time forth stay in this town. More than this, he hath not felt dread to rail on you, my lord, who are now sent to be his judge."

When this Pickthank had told his tale, the judge spoke to the man at the bar, and said, "Thou vile, base wretch, hast thou heard what those just and true men have sworn to thy bane?"

Fai.—"I say then, as a set off to what Mr. Envy hath said, I spoke not a word but this, 'That what rule, or laws, or rights, or men, are flat down on the Word of God, are foes to the faith of Christ.'

"As to the next, to wit, Mr. Superstition, and his charge to my hurt, I said but this, 'That to serve God one needs a faith from on high; but there can be no faith from on high void of the will of God made known from the same source. Hence, all that is thrust on us that does not square with this will of God, is but of man's faith; which faith will not serve the life that is to come.'

"As to what Mr. Pickthank hath said, 'That the prince of this town, with all the roughs, his slaves, are more fit for one in hell than in this town and land'; and so the Lord be good to me."

Then the judge said to those who were to bind or loose him from the charge: "Ye who serve here to weigh this case, you see this man of whom so great a din hath been made in this town. It doth lie now on your souls to hang him, or save his life; but yet I think meet to teach you a few points of our law.

"There was an act made in the days of Pharaoh the great, friend to our prince, that, lest those of a wrong faith should spread and grow too strong for him, their males should be thrown in the stream. There was, in like way, an act made in the days of Nebuchadnezzar the great, who, too, did serve him, that such as would not fall down and laud the form he had set up, should be flung in a pit of

Then stood forth Envy and said: "My lord, this man in spite
of his fair name, is one of the most vile men in our land."—
Page 61.   *Pilgrim's Progress.*

fire. Now the pith of these laws this rogue has set at naught, not in mere thought but in word and deed as well. Twice, nay thrice, he speaks of our creed as a thing of naught; and for this, on his own words, he needs must die the death."

Then went out those who had to weigh the case, whose names were Mr. Blind-man, Mr. No-good, Mr. Malice, Mr. Love-lust, Mr. Live-loose, Mr. Heady, Mr. High-mind, Mr. Enmity, Mr. Liar, Mr. Cruelty, Mr. Hate-light, and Mr. Implacable; who each one gave in his voice to Faithful's hurt, in his own mind; and then meant to make known his doom in face of the judge. And Mr. Blindman, the chief, said, " I see, most plain, that this man is a foe; let us at once doom him to death. And so they did. The judge then put on the black cap, and said, " That he should be led from the place where he was to the place from whence he came, and there to be put to the worst death that could be thought off."

They then brought him out to do with him as the law set forth: and first they whipt him; then they did pelt him with stones; and, last of all, they burnt him to dust at the stake. Thus came Faithful to his end.

Now I saw that there stood in the rear of the crowd a state car, with two steeds, that did wait for Faithful; who, as soon as his foes had got rid of him, was caught up in it and straight sent off through the clouds, with sound of trump, the most near way to the Celestial Gate. But as for Christian, he was put back to jail; so there he lay for a space: but He that rules all things, in whose hand was the might of their rage, so wrought it that Christian, for that time got free from them and went his way,

CHAPTER XIV.

CHRISTIAN AND HOPEFUL.

Now I saw in my dream that Christian went not forth with none to cheer him; for there was one whose name was Hopeful, who set out with him, and made a grave pact that he would be his friend.

So I saw that when they were just got out of the fair they came up with one that had gone on in front of them, whose name was By-ends. He told them that he came from the town of Fair-speech, and was bound for the Celestial City; but he told them not his name.

Chr.—" Pray, sir, what may I call you?"

By.—" I know not you, nor you me: if you mean to go this way, I shall be glad to go with you: if not, I must take things as they come."

Then Christian stept on one side to his friend Hopeful, and said, "It runs in my mind that this is one By-ends, of Fair-speech, and if it be he, we have as keen a knave in our midst as dwells in all these parts." Then said Hopeful, "Ask him; I think he should not blush at his name." So Christian came up with him once more, and said, "Sir, is not your name Mr. By-ends, of Fair-speech?"

By.—" This is not my name; but, in sooth, it is a name I got in scorn from some that do not like me."

Chr.—" I thought, in sooth, that you were the man that I had heard of; and, to tell you what I think, I fear this name suits you more than you would wish we should think it doth."

By.—" Well, if you will thus think, I durst not help it:

HOPEFUL joins company with CHRISTIAN

you shall find me a fair man, if you will make me one of you."

Chr.—" If you will go with us, you must go in the teeth of wind and tide ; you must, in like wise, own Faith in his rags, as well as when in his sheen shoes ; and stand by him, too, when bound in chains, as well as when he walks the streets with praise."

By.—" You must not curb my faith, nor lord it in this way : leave me free to think, and let me go with you."

Chr.—" Not a step more, save you will do in what I shall speak as we."

Then said By-ends, " I shall not cast off my old views, since they bring no harm, and are of use. If I may not go with you, I must do as I did ere you came up with me, that is, go on with no one, till some will come on who will be glad to meet me."

Now I saw in my dream that Christian and Hopeful left him, and went on in front of him : but one of them did chance to look back, and saw three men in the wake of Mr. By-ends, and lo, as they came up with him, he made them quite a low bow. The men's names were Mr. Hold-the-world, Mr. Money-love, and Mr. Save-all ; men that Mr. By-ends had erst known ; for when boys they were mates at school, and were taught by one Mr. Gripeman, who keeps a school in Love-gain, which is a large town in the shire of Coveting, in the north.

Well, when they, as I said, did greet in turn, Mr. Money-love said to Mr. By-ends, " Who are they on the road right in front of us ? "

By.—" They are a pair from a land far off, that, in their mode, are bent on a long route."

Money.—" Ah ! why did they not stay ; that we might

Then Christian saw three men in the wake of Mr. By-ends, and lo, as they came up with him he made them a very low bow.—Page 66.

Pilgrim's Progress.

have gone on with them? for they, and we, and you, sir, I hope, are all bent on the same road."

By.—"Why, they, in their fierce mood, think that they are bound to rush on their way at all times; while I wait for wind and tide. They like to risk all for God at a clap; while I like to seize all means to make safe my life and lands. They are for Faith when in rags and scorn; but I am for him when he walks in his sheen shoes in the sun, and with praise."

Hold.—"Ay, and hold you there still, good Mr. By-ends: for my part I can count him but a fool, that with the means to keep what he has, he shall be so lack of sense as to lose it. For my part, I like that faith best that will stand with the pledge of God's good gifts to us. Abraham and Solomon grew rich in faith: and Job says that a good man 'shall lay up gold as dust.' But he must not be such as the men in front of us, if they be as you have said of them."

Save.—"I think that we are all of one mind in this thing; and hence there need no more words be said of it."

Mr. By-ends and his friends did lag and keep back, that Christian and Hopeful might go on in front of them.

Then Christian and Hopeful went till they came to a nice plain known as Ease; which did please them much: but that plain was but strait, so they were soon got through it. Now at the far side of that plain was a small hill, which went by the name of Lucre, and in that hill a gold mine, which some of them that had been that way had gone on one side to see; but, as they got too near the brink of the pit, the ground, as it was not sound, broke when they trod on it, and they were slain.

Then I saw in my dream that a short way off the road,

nigh to the gold mine, stood Demas, a man of fair looks,
to call to such as went that way to come and see; who
said to Christian and his friend, "Ho! turn hence on this
side, and I will show you a thing. Here is a gold mine,
and some that dig in it for wealth: if you will come, with

DEMAS TEMPTS CHRISTIAN AND HOPEFUL.

slight pains you may gain a rich store for your use."

Then Christian did call to Demas, and said, "Is not the
way rife with risks? Hath it not let some in their way?"

Dem.—"Not so much so, save to those that take no
care." But a blush came on his face as he spake.

Then said Christian to Hopeful, "Let us not stir a step, but still keep on our way."

By this time By-ends and those who were with him came once more in sight, and they, at the first beck, went straight to Demas. Now, that they fell in the pit, as they stood on the brink of it, or that they went down to dig, or that they lost their breath at the base by the damps that, as a rule, rise from it, of these things I am not sure; but this I saw, that from that time forth they were not seen once more in the way. Which strange sight gave them cause for grave talk.

CHAPTER XV.

DOUBTING CASTLE AND GIANT DESPAIR.

I SAW then, that they went on their way to a fair stream. Here then Christian and his friend did walk with great joy. They drank, too, of the stream, which was sweet to taste, and like balm to their faint hearts. More than this, on the banks of this stream, on each side, were green trees with all kinds of fruit: and the leaves they ate to ward off ills that come of too much food and heat of blood, while on the way. On each side of the stream was a mead, bright with white plants; and it was green all the year long. In this mead they lay down and slept. When they did wake they felt a wish to go on, and set out. Now the way from the stream was rough, and their feet soft, for that they came a long road: so the souls of the men were sad, from the state of the way. Now, not far in front of them, there was on the left hand of the road a mead, and a stile to get right to it: and that mead is known as By-path Meadow. Then said Christian to his friend, "If this mead doth lie close by the side of our way, let us go straight to it." Then said Christian to his friends, "If this mead doth lie close by the side of our way, let us go straight to it." Then he went to the stile to see, and lo, a path lay close by the way on the far off side of the fence. "It is just as I wish," said Christian; "come, good Hopeful, and let us cross to it."

Hope.—"But how if this path should lead us out of the way?"

"That is not like to be," said the next. "Look, doth it not go straight on by the side of the way?" So Hopeful, when he thought on what his friend said, went in his steps, and did cross the stile; and at the same time, while they cast their eyes in front of them, they saw a man that did walk as they did, and his name was Vain-Confidence: so they did call to him, and ask him to what place that way led. He said, "To the Celestial Gate." "Look," said Christian, "did not I tell you so? by this you may see we are right." So they went in his wake, and he went in front of them. But, lo, the night came on, and it grew quite dark; so that they that were in the rear lost the sight of him that went in front.

He then that went in front, as he did not see the way clear, fell in a deep pit, which was there made by the prince of those grounds to catch such vain fools with the rest, and was torn in bits by his fall.

Now Christian and his friend heard him fall: so they did call to know the cause: but there was none to speak.

Then Hopeful gave a deep groan, and said, "Oh, that I had kept on my way!"

Chr.—"Good friend, do not feel hurt. I grieve I have

This is Vain Confidence, whom Christian and Hopeful saw in
the way as they did walk.-- Page 70   *Pilgrim's Progress.*

brought thee out of the way, and that I have put thee in no slight strait; pray, my friend, let this pass; I did not do it of a bad will."

Hope.—"Be of good cheer, my friend, for I give thee shrift; and trust, too, this shall be for our good."

Then, so as to cheer them, they heard the voice of one that said, "Let thine heart be set on the high road; and the way that thou didst go turn once more." But by this time the way that they should go back was rife with risk. Then I thought that we get more quick out of the way when we are in it, than in it when we are out.

Nor could they, with all the skill they had, get once more to the stile that night. For which cause, as they at last did light neath a slight shed, they sat down there till day broke: but as they did tire they fell to sleep. Now there was not far from the place where they lay a fort, known as Doubting Castle, and he who kept it was Giant Despair: and it was on his grounds that they now slept. Hence, as he got up at dawn, and did walk up and down in his fields, he caught Christian and Hopeful in sound sleep on his grounds. They told him they were poor wights, and that they had lost their way. Then said the Giant, "You have this night come where you should not; you did tramp in, and lie on, my grounds, and so you must go hence with me." So they were made to go, for that he had more strength than they. They, too, had but few words to say, for they knew they were in a fault. The Giant hence drove them in front of him, and put them in his fort, in a dank, dark cell, that was foul and stunk to the souls of these two men. Here then they lay for full four days, and had not one bit of bread, or drop of drink, or light, or one to ask how they did: they were, hence, here in bad case, and were far from friends and all who knew them. Now in this place Christian had more than his own share of grief, for it was through his bad words that they were brought to such dire bale.

Now Giant Despair had a wife, and her name was Diffidence: so when he was gone to bed he told his wife what he had done. Then he did ask her, too, what he had best do more to them. Then she said to him that when he got up in the morn he should beat them, and show no ruth. So when he rose he gets him a huge stick of crab, and goes down to the cell to them, and falls on them and beats them in such sort that they could do naught to ward off his blows, or to turn them on the floor. This done, he goes off and leaves them there to soothe each one his friend, and to mourn their grief. The next night, she spoke with her lord more as to their case, and when she found that they were not dead, did urge him to tell them to take their own lives. So when morn was come he told them that since they were not like to come out of that place, their best way would be at once to put an end to their lives, with knife, rope, or drug. But they did pray him to let them go; with that he gave a frown on them, ran at them, and had no doubt made an end of them with his own hand, but that he fell in one of his fits. From which cause he went off, and left them to think what to do. Then did the men talk of the best course to take; and thus they spoke:

"Friend," said Christian, "what shall we do? The life that we now live is fraught with ill: for my part, I know not if it be best to live thus, or die out of hand: the grave has more ease for me than this cell."

Hope.—"Of a truth, our state is most dread, and death

would be more of a boon to me than thus hence to stay: but let us not take our own lives." With these words Hopeful then did soothe the mind of his friend: so they did stay each with each in the dark that day, in their sad and drear plight.

Well, as dusk came on the Giant goes down to the cell once more, to see if those he held bound there had done as he had bid them: but when he came there he found they still did live, at which he fell in a great rage, and told them that, as he saw they had lent a deaf ear to what he said, it should be worse for them than if they had not been born.

At this they shook with dread, and I think that Christian fell in a swoon; but as he came round once more, they took up the same strain of speech as to the Giant's words, and if it were best give heed to them or no. Now Christian once more did seem to wish to yield, but Hopeful made his next speech in this wise:

"My friend," said he, "dost thou not know how brave thou hast been in times past? The foul fiend could not crush thee; nor could all that thou didst hear, or see, or feel in the Vale of the Shade of Death; what wear and tear, grief and fright, hast thou erst gone through, and art thou naught but fears? Thou dost see that I am in the cell with thee, and I am a far more weak man to look at than thou art: in like way, this Giant did wound me as well as thee, and hath, too, cut off the bread and drink from my mouth, and with thee I mourn void of the light. But let us try and grow more strong: call to mind how thou didst play the man at Vanity Fair, and wast not made blench at the chain or cage, nor yet at fierce death; for which cause let us, at least to shun the shame that

looks not well for a child of God to be found in, bear up
with calm strength as well as we can."

Now night had come once more, and his wife spoke to
him of the men, and sought to know if they had done as
he had told them. To which he said, "They are stout
rogues; they choose the more to bear all hard things than
to put an end to their lives." Then said she, "Take them
to the garth next day, and show them the bones and skulls
of those that thou hast put to death, and make them think
thou wilt tear them in shreds, as thou hast done to folk
like to them."

So when the morn was come the Giant takes them to
the garth, and shows them as his wife had bade him:
"These," said he, "were wights, as you are, once, and
they trod on my ground, as you have done; and when I
thought fit I tore them in bits, and so in the space of ten
days I will do you: go, get you down to your den once
more." And with that he beat them all the way to the
place. They lay for this cause all day in a sad state, just
as they had done. Now, when night was come, and when
Mrs. Diffidence and her spouse the Giant were got to bed,
they once more spoke of the men; and, with this, the Giant
thought it strange that he could not by his blows or words
bring them to an end. And with that his wife said, "I
fear that they live in hopes that some will come to set
them free, or that they have things to pick locks with them,
by the means of which they hope to scape." "And dost
thou say so, my dear?" said the Giant; "I will hence
search them in the morn."

Well, in the depth of night they strove hard to pray,
and held it up till just break of day.

Now, not long ere it was day, good Christian, as one

CHRISTIAN&HOPEFUL escape from DOUBTING CASTLE.

half wild, brake out in this hot speech: "What a fool," quoth he, " am I, thus to lie in a foul den when I may as well walk in the free air: I have a key in my breast known as Promise, that will, I feel sure, pick each lock in Doubting Castle." Then said Hopeful, "That is good news, my friend; pluck it out of thy breast and try."

Then Christian took it out of his breast, and did try at the cell door, whose bolt as he did turn the key gave back, and the door flew back with ease, and Christian and Hopeful both came out. Then he went to the front door that leads to the yard of the fort, and with this key did ope that door in like way. Then he went to the brass gate (for that he must ope too), but that lock he had hard work to move; yet did the key pick it. Then they thrust wide the gate to make their scape with speed. But that gate as it went back did creak so, that it woke Giant Despair, who, as he rose in haste to go in search of the men, felt his limbs to fail, for his fits took him once more, so that he could by no means go in their track. Then they went on, and came to the King's high road once more, and so were safe, for that they were out of his grounds.

Now, when they had got clear of the stile, they thought in their minds what they should do at that stile, to keep those that should come in their wake from the fell hands of Giant Despair. So their built there a pile and wrote on the side of it these words: "To cross this stile is the way to Doubting Castle, which is kept by Giant Despair, who spurns the King of the good land, and seeks to kill such as serve him."

CHAPTER XVI.

THE DELECTABLE MOUNTAINS.

THEY went then till they came to the Delectable Mountains, which mounts the Lord of that hill doth own of whom we erst did speak : so they went up to the mounts, to see the plants, trees rife with fruit, the vines and founts ; where, too, they drank, did wash, and eat of the grapes till no gust was left for more. Now there were on the top of these mounts, Shepherds that fed their flocks, and they stood by the side of the high road. Christian and Hopeful then went to them, and while they leant on their staves (as is the case with wights who tire when they stand to talk with folk by the way), they said, " Whose Delectable Mountains are these ? and whose be the sheep that fed on them ? "

Shep.—" These mounts are Immanuel's Land, and they can be seen from this town : and the sheep in like way are his, and he laid down his life for them."

Chr.—" Is this the way to the Celestial City ? "

Shep.—" You are just in your way."

I saw, too, in my dream that when the Shepherds saw that they were men on the road, they in like way did ask them things, to which they spoke, as was their wont : as, " Whence came you ? and how got you in the way ? and by what means have you so held on in it ? for but few of them that set out to come hence do show their face on these mounts." But when the Shepherds heard their speech, which did please them, they gave them looks of love, and said, "Good come with thee to the Mounts of Joy."

The Shepherds, I say, whose names were Knowledge, Experience, Watchful, and Sincere, took them by the hand and had them to their tents, and made them eat and drink of that which was there at the time. They said, too, " We would that you should stay here a short time, to get known to us, and yet more to cheer your heart with the good of these Mounts of Joy." They told them that they would much like to stay; and so they went to their rest that night, for that it was so late.

Then I saw in my dream, that in the morn the Shepherds did call on Christian and Hopeful to walk with them on the mounts. Then said the Shepherds, each to his friend, " Shall we show these wights with staves some strange sights?" So they had them first to the top of a hill, known as Error, and bid them look down to the base. So Christian and Hopeful did look down, and saw at the foot a lot of men rent all to bits, by a fall that they had from the top. Then said Christian, "What doth this mean?" The Shepherds said, " Have you not heard of them that were made to err, in that they gave heed to Hymeneus and Philetus, who held not the faith that the dead shall rise from the grave? Those that you see lie rent in bits at the base of this mount are they; and they have lain to this day on the ground as you see, so that those who come this way may take heed how they climb too high, or how they come too near the brink of this mount."

Then I saw that they had them to the top of the next mount, and the name of that is Caution, and bid them look as far off as they could; which when they did they saw, as they thought, a group of men that did walk up and down through the tombs that were there: and they saw that the men were blind, for that they fell at times on the tombs, and for that they could not get out from the midst of them. Then said Christian, "What means this?"

The Shepherds then said, "Did you not see, a short way

THE HILL ERROR.

down these mounts, a stile that leads to a mead on the left hand of this way?" They said, "Yes." Then said the Shepherds, "From that stile there goes a path that leads straight to Doubting Castle, which is kept by Giant Despair, and these men (as he did point to them in the

midst of the tombs) came once on the way, as you do now
—ay, till they came to that same stile!　And as they found
the right way was rough in that place, they chose to go
out of it to that mead, and there were caught by Giant
Despair and shut up in Doubting Castle; where, when
they had a while been kept in a cell, he at last did put out
their eyes, and led them in the thick of those tombs, where
he has left them to stray till this day: that the words of
the Wise Man might be brought to pass, 'He that strays
out of the way of truth shall dwell in the homes of the
dead.'"　Then did Christian and Hopeful look each on
each, while tears came from their eyes; but yet said they
not a word to the Shepherds.

Then I saw in my dream, that the Shepherds had them
to one more place, in a steep, where was a door in the side
of a hill; and they flung wide the door and bid them look
in.　They did look in, hence, and saw that it was dark and
full of smoke; they thought, too, that they heard a hoarse
noise, as of fire, and a cry of some in pain.　Then said
Christian, "What means this?"　The Shepherds told them,
"This is a nigh way to Hell; a way that such as seem to
be what they are not go in at: to wit, such as sell the right
they had at birth, with Esau; such as sell their Lord, with
Judas; such as speak ill of God's Word, with Alexander;
and that lie and shift, with Ananias, and Sapphira his
wife."

Then said Hopeful to the Shepherds, "I see that these
had on them, each one, a show of the road, as we have
now, had they not?"

Shep.—"Yes, and held it a long time too."

Hope.—"How far might they go on in the way, in their
days, since they, in spite of this, were thus cast off?"

Shep.—" Some yon, and some not so far as these mounts."

By this time Christian and Hopeful had a wish to go forth, and the Shepherds meant that they should : so they sped side by side till they got nigh the end of the mounts. Then said the Shepherds, each to his friend, " Let us here show these wights the gates of the Celestial City, if they have skill to look through our kind of glass." The men then did like the hint : so they had them to the top of a high hill, the name of which was Clear, and gave them the glass to look.

Then did they try to look, but the thought of that last thing that the Shepherds had shown them made their hands shake ; by means of which let they could not look well through the glass ; yet they thought they saw a thing like the gate, and, in like way, some of the sheen of the place.

Just ere they set out, one of the Shepherds gave them *a note of the way ;* the next bid them *take heed of such as fawn ;* the third bid them *take heed that they slept not on ground that had a spell ;* and the fourth bid them **God** speed. So I did wake from my dream.

CHAPTER XVII.

THE ENCHANTED GROUND AND THE WAY DOWN TO IT.

AND I slept and dreamt once more, and saw the same two wights go down the mounts, by the high road that led to the town. Now nigh the base of these mounts, on the left hand, lies the land of Conceit, from which land there comes, right in the way in which the men trod, a small lane with twists and turns. Here, then, they met with a brisk lad that came out of that land, and his name was Ignorance. So Christian would know from what parts he came, and whence he was bound.

Ignor.—" Sir, I was born in the land that lies off there a short way on the left hand, and I am bound to the Celestial City."

Chr.—" But how do you think to get in at the gate? for you may find some let there."

" As some good folk do," said he.

Chr.—" But what have you to show at that gate, that the gate should be flung wide to you?"

Ignor.—" I know my Lord's will, and have led a good life; I pay each man his own; I pray, fast, pay tithes, and give alms; and have left my land for the place to which I go."

Chr.—" But thou didst not come in at the Wicket-gate that is at the head of this way; thou didst come in here through that same lane with the twists and turns; and hence, I fear, in spite of what thou dost think of thy right, when the last day shall come, thou wilt have laid to thy charge that thou art a thief, in lieu of a free pass to the town."

Ignor.—" Sirs, ye be not known to me in the least; I know you not; you be led by the faith of your land, and I will be led by the faith of mine. I hope all will be well. And as for the gate that you talk of, all the world knows that that is a great way off our land. I do not think that one man in all our parts doth so much as know the way to it; nor need they care if they do or no; since we have, as you see, a fine, gay, green lane, that comes down from our land, the next road that leads to the way."

Then Christian met with a brisk lad who said his name was
Ignorance.—Page 82.   *Pilgrim's Prog. 82.*

When Christian saw that the man was wise in his own eyes, he said to Hopeful in a soft voice, " 'There is more hope of a fool than of him'"; and said, in like way, " 'When he that is a fool walks by the way, his sense fails him, and he saith to each one that he is a fool.' What! shall we talk more with him, or move on now, and so leave him to think of what he hath erst heard, and then stop once more for him in a while, and see if by slow steps we can do aught of good to him?" Then said Hopeful, "It is not good, I think, to say so to him all at once; let us pass him by, if you will, and talk to him by and by, just as he has 'strength to bear it.'"

So they both went on, and Ignorance came in their track. Now, when they had left him a short way, they came to a dark lane, where they met a man whom some fiends had bound with strong cords, and took back to the door that they saw on the side of the hill. Now good Christian could not help but shake, and so did Hopeful, who was with him; yet, as the fiends led off the man, Christian did look to see if he knew him; and he thought it might be one Turnaway, that dwelt in the town of Apostacy. But he did not well see his face, for he did hang his head like a thief that is found. But when he had gone past, Hopeful gave a look at him, and saw on his back a card, with these words, "Vile cheat, that has left his faith."

So they went on, and Ignorance went in their track. They went till they came at a place where they saw a way put right in their way, and did seem, at the same time, to lie as straight as the way which they should go. And here they knew not which of the two to take, for both did seem straight in front of them: hence they stood to think. And as they thought of the way, lo a man black of flesh, but clad with a light robe, came to them, and did ask them why they stood there. They said they were bound to the Celestial City, but knew not which of these ways to take. "Go with me," said the man; "it is to that place I am bent." So they went with him in the way that but now came to the road, which each step they took did turn and turn them so far from the town that they sought to go to, that in a short time their heads did turn off from it; yet they went with him. But by and by, ere they well knew of it, he led them both in the bounds of a net, in which they were both so caught that they knew not what to do; and with that the white robe fell off the black man's back: then they saw where they were. For which cause there they lay in tears some time, for they could not get their limbs out.

Then said Christian to his friend, "Now do I see that I am wrong. Did not the Shepherds bid us take heed of the Flatterer? As are the words of the Wise Man, so we have found it this day, 'A man that fawns on his friend spreads a net for his feet.'"

Hope.—"They, too, gave us some notes as to the way, so that we may be the more sure to find it; but in that we have not thought to read."

Thus they lay in sad plight in the net. At last they saw a Bright One come nigh to where they were, with a whip of small cords in his hand. When he was come to the place where they were, he did ask them whence they came, and what they did there? They told him they were poor wights bound to Zion, but were led out of their way by a black man clad in white, "who bid us," said they, "go with him, for he was bound to that place too." Then said he with the whip. "It is one who fawns, a false guide

Then did Hopeful tell Christian his experience, and Christian said: "Let us not sleep, as some do, but let us watch and pray."
—Page 86.

Pilgrim's Progress.

who wore the garb of a sprite of light." So he rent the net, and let the men out. Then said he to them, "Come with me, that I may set you in your way once more": so he led them back to the way they had left to go with the Flatterer. Then he did ask them and said, "Where did you lie the last night?" They said, "With the Shepherds on the Mounts of Joy." He did ask, then, if they had not of those men a note as a guide for the way. They said, "Yes." "But did you not," said he, "when you were at a stand, pluck out and read your note?" Quoth they, "No." He did ask them, "Why?" They said, "They did not think of it." He would know, too, "If the Shepherds did not bid them take heed of the Flatterer?" They said, "Yes; but we thought not," said they, "that this man of fine speech had been he."

Then I saw in my dream that he told them to lie down; which when they did, he gave them sore stripes, to teach them the good way in which they should walk. This done, he bids them go on their way, and take good heed to the next hints of the Shepherds.

I then saw in my dream, that they went on till they came to a land whose air did tend to make one sleep. And here Hopeful grew quite dull and nigh fell to sleep: for which cause he said to Christian: "I do now grow so dull that I can scarce hold ope mine eyes; let us lie down here and take one nap."

"By no means," said Christian, "lest if we sleep we wake not more."

Hope.—"Why, my friend? Sleep is sweet to the man that toils: it may give us strength if we take a nap."

Chr.—"Do you not know that one of the Shepherds bid us take heed of the Enchanted Ground? He meant

by that, that we should take care and not go to sleep.
'Let us not sleep, as do some; but let us watch and be of
sound mind.'"

Hope.—"I know I am in fault; and, had not you been
with me here, I had gone to sleep and run the risk of

HOPEFUL TELLS CHRISTIAN HIS EXPERIENCE.

death. I see it is true that the wise man saith, 'Two are
more good than one.' Up to this time thou hast been my
ruth; and thou shalt 'have a good meed for thy pains.'"

I saw then in my dream, that Hopeful gave a look back,
and saw Ignorance, whom they had left in their wake,
come in their track. "Look," said he to Christian, "how
far yon youth doth lag in the rear."

"Come on, man, why do you stay back so?" said Christian.
"I like to walk alone," said Ignorance.—Page 87.

Chr.—"Ay, ay, I see him: he cares not to be with us."

Hope.—"But I trow it would not have hurt him had he kept pace with us to this time."

Chr.—"That is true: but I wot he doth not think so."

Hope.—"That I think he doth: but, be it so or no, let us wait for him." So they did.

Then Christian did call to him, "Come you on, man: why do you stay back so?"

Ignor.—"I like to walk in this lone way; ay, more a great deal than with folk: that is, save I like them much."

Then said Christian to Hopeful (but in a soft voice), "Did I not tell you he sought to shirk us? But, be this as it may, come up, and let us talk off the time in this lone place."

Then, when he had a long speech with Ignorance, Christian spoke thus to his friend, "Well, come, my good Hopeful, I see that thou and I must walk side by side once more."

So I saw in my dream, that they went on fast in front, and Ignorance, he came with lame gait in their track. Then said Christian to his friend, "I feel much for this poor man: it will of a truth go hard with him at last."

CHAPTER XVIII.

THE LAND OF BEULAH—THE FORDS OF THE RIVER— AT HOME.

Now I saw in my dream that by this time the wights had got clear of the Enchanted Ground, and had come to the land of Beulah, whose air was most sweet: as the way did lie straight through it, they took rest there for a while.

Yea, here they heard at all times "the songs of birds," and saw each day the plants bud forth in the earth, and heard "the voice of the dove" in the land. In this realm the sun shines night and day : for this was far from the Vale of the Shade of Death, and, in like way, out of the

CHRISTIAN AND HOPEFUL ENTER THE LAND OF BEULAH.

reach of Giant Despair ; nor could they from this place so much as see Doubting Castle. Here they were in sight of the City to which they were bound : here, too, met them some of the folk who dwelt there, for in this land the Bright Ones did walk, for that it was on the verge of bliss.

Now as they did walk in this land they had more joy than in parts not so nigh the realm to which they were bound: and as they drew near the City they had yet a more clear view of it. It was built of pearls and rare gems: its streets, too, were of gold: so that, from the sheen of the place, and the glow of the sun on it, Christian did long so much that he fell sick. Hopeful, in like way, had a fit or two of the same kind.

But when they got some strength, and could bear their sick state, they went on their way, and came near and yet more near where were grounds that bore fruits, vines, and plants; and their gates did ope on the high road. Now, as they came up to these parts, lo, the Gardener stood in the way; to whom the men said, "Whose fine vine and fruit grounds are these?" He said, "They are the King's, and are put there for his own joy, as well as to cheer such as come this way." So he took them to where the vines grew, and bid them wet their mouths with the fruit: he, too, did show them there the King's walks, and the shades that he sought: and here they staid and slept.

Now I saw in my dream that they spoke more in their sleep at this time than erst they did in all their way: and as I did muse on it, the Gardener said to me, "Why dost thou muse at this? It is a charm in the fruit of the grapes of these grounds ' to go down in so sweet a way as to cause the lips of them that sleep to speak.'"

So I saw that when they did wake they girt up their loins to go up to the City. So as they went on, there met them two men in robes that shone like gold, while the face of each was bright as the light.

These men did ask them whence they came; and they told them. They would know, too, where they did lodge, and what straits and risks and joys they had met with in the way; and they told them. Then said the men that met them, " You have but two straits more to meet with, and then you are in the City."

Christian then, and his friend, did ask the men to go with them: so they told them that they would; but said they, " You must gain it by your own faith." So I saw in my dream that they went on each with each, till they came in sight of the gate.

Now I saw still more, that a stream ran in front of them and the gate; but there was no bridge to cross, and the stream was deep. At the sight of this stream, the wights with staves took fright; but the men that went with them said, " Thou must go through, or thou canst not come at the gate."

The wights then sought to know if there was no way but that to the gate. To which they said, " Yes; but none, save two—to wit, Enoch and Elijah—hath been let to tread that path since the world was made, nor shall till the last trump shall sound." The wights then (and Christian in chief) grew as if they would give up hope, and did look this way and that, but no way could be found by which they might get clear of the stream. Then they did ask the men if it was all the same depth. They said, " No "; yet they could not help them in that case: " for," said they, " you shall find it more or less deep as you trust in the King of the place."

Then they did wade in the stream, and as Christian sank he did cry to his good friend Hopeful, and said, " I sink."

Then said Hopeful, " Be of good cheer, my friend: I feel the ground, and it is good. Then said Christian, " Ah! my friend, I shall not see the land I seek." And

with that all grew dark, and fear fell on Christian, so that he could not see in front of him. All the words that he spoke still did tend to show that he had dread of mind and fears of heart that he should die in that stream, and fail to go in at the gate. Hopeful, from this cause, had here hard work to hold up the head of his friend; yea, at times he would be quite gone down, and then, ere a while, he would rise up once more half dead. Hopeful would try to cheer him, and said, "Friend, I see the gate, and men stand by to greet us": but Christian would say, "'Tis you, 'tis you they wait for; you have had hope since the time I knew you." Then said Hopeful, "These fears and griefs that you go through are no sign that God has left you, but are sent to try you; if you will call to mind that which of yore you have had from him, and live on him in your griefs."

Then I saw in my dream that Christian was in a muse for a while. To whom, too, Hopeful did add these words, "Be of good cheer, Christ doth make thee whole." And with that Christian brake out with a loud voice, "Oh, I see Him once more! and he tells me, 'When thou dost pass through the stream, I will be with thee.'" Then they both took heart, and the foe then grew as still as a stone, till they were gone through. Christian then straight found ground to stand on, and so it came to pass that the rest of the stream was but of slight depth: thus they did ford it.

Now on the bank of the stream, on the far off side, they saw the two Bright Men once more, who there did wait for them. When they came out of the stream these did greet them, and said: "We are sprites sent forth to aid them who shall be heirs of Christ." Thus they went on to the gate.

Now you must note that the City stood on a high hill:

but the wights went up that hill with ease, for that they had these two men to lead them up by the arms: more than this, they had left the garb they wore in the stream; for though they went in with them they came out freed from them. They hence went up here with much speed, though the rise on which the City was built was more high than the clouds. They then went up through the realms of air, and held sweet talk as they went, as they felt joy for that they had got safe through the stream, and had such Bright Ones to wait them.

The talk that they had with the Bright Ones was of the place; who told them that no words could paint it. "You go now," said they, "to the sphere where God dwells, in which you shall see the Tree of Life, and eat of the fruits of it that fade not: and when you come there you shall have white robes to wear, and your walk and talk shall be each day with the King, while time shall be known no more. There you shall not see such things as you saw when low on earth, to wit, grief, pain, and death; for these things are gone. You now go to Abraham, to Isaac, and Jacob, and to men that God 'took from the woe to come.'" These men then did ask, "What must we do in this pure place?" To whom it was said, "You must there get the meed of all your toil, and have joy for all your grief; you must reap what you have sown, ay, the fruit of all your tears and toils for the King by the way. In that place you must wear crowns of gold, and bask for aye in the sight of the Lord of Hosts, for there you 'shall see Him as he is.' There, too, you shall serve Him with praise, with shouts, with joy, whom you sought to serve in the world, though with much pain, for that your flesh was weak. There you shall join with your friends once more that are gone there ere you; and there you shall with joy greet each one that comes in your wake. When the King shall come with sound of trump in the clouds, as on the wings of the wind, you shall come with Him; and, when He shall sit on the Throne to judge all the realms of the earth, you shall sit by Him: yea, and when He shall pass doom on all that did work ill, let them be sprites or men, you shall too have a voice in that doom, for that they are His and your foes. More than this, when He shall go back to the City, you shall go too, with sound of trump, and be for aye with Him."

Now while they thus drew nigh to the gate, lo a troop of the Bright Host came to meet them; to whom it was said by the first two Bright Ones, "These are the men that did love our Lord, when they were in the world, and that have left all for His name, and He hath sent us to fetch them, and we have brought them thus far on their way, that they may go in and look their Lord in the face with joy." There came, too, at this time to meet them a group of the King's men with trumps, clad in white and sheen robes, who, with sweet and loud notes, made the whole arch of the sky full of the sound. These men did greet Christian and his friend with much warmth; and this they did with shouts and sound of trump.

This done, they went round them on each side; some went in front, some in the rear, and some on the right hand, some on the left (as it were to guard them through the vast realms), and did sound as they went, with sweet noise, in notes on high; so that the bare sight was to them that could look on it as if all the blest were come down to meet them. Thus then did they walk on side by side. And now were these two men, as it were, in bliss ere they

" 'Tis you, 'tis you they wait for; you have had hope since the
time I knew you."

(The Pilgrim's Progress.)

came at it. Here, too, they had the City in view; and
they thought they heard all the bells in it to ring, so as to
greet them. But, more than all, the warm and rare
thoughts that they had of the place to which they went,
and of those that dwelt there, and that for aye; oh! by
what tongue or pen can such vast joy be told? Thus they
came up to the gate.

Then I saw in my dream that the Bright Men bid them
call at the gate: the which when they did, some from on
high did look down, to wit, Enoch, Moses, and Elijah, and
so forth, to whom it was said, " These wights are come
from the City of Destruction, for the love that they bear
to the King of this place "; and then the wights gave in to
them each man his roll, which they had got at first: those,
then, were brought in to the King, who, when he had read
them, said, " Where are the men? " To whom it was told,
" They are at the porch of the gate." Then spoke the
King, " Ope the gate, that the just land that keeps truth
may come in."

Now I saw in my dream, that these two men went in at
the gate: and lo! as they did so, a change came on them;
and they had robes put on that shone like gold. There
were, too, that met them with harps and crowns, and gave
them to them; the harps to praise with, the crowns in sign
of rank. Then I heard in my dream that all the bells of
the place rang for joy, and that it was said to them, "Come
ye to the joy of our Lord."

Now, just as the gates did ope to let in the men, did I
peer at them, and lo, the place shone like the sun: the
streets, too, were of gold; and in them did walk men
with crowns on their heads, palms in their hands, and gold
harps to aid in songs of praise

There were some of them that had wings, and they sang, with not a pause, songs to the " Lamb that was slain ! "

Then they shut up the gates ; which when I had seen I did wish to be with them.

Now, while I did gaze on all these things, I saw Ignorance come up to the side of the stream : but he soon got through, and that void of half the toil which the two men that I of late saw met with. So he did climb the hill to come up to the gate ; but none came with him, nor did one man meet or greet him. When he was come up to the gate, he gave a look up at what was writ in front of it, and then gave a knock. So they told the King, but he would not come down to see him ; but told the two Bright Ones, that led Christian and Hopeful to the City, to go out and take Ignorance, and bind him hand and foot, and have him off. Then they took him up, and bore him through the air to the door that I saw in the side of the hill, and put him in there. Then I saw that there was a way to Hell, ay, from the gates of bliss, as well as from the City of Destruction ! So I did wake, and lo, it was a dream !

THE END.

BURT'S SERIES of ONE SYLLABLE BOOKS

14 Titles. Handsome Illuminated Cloth Binding.

A series of Classics, selected specially for young people's reading, and told in simple language for youngest readers. Printed from large type, with many illustrations.

Price 65 Cents per Volume.

Aesop's Fables.
Retold in words of one syllable for young people. By MARY GODOLPHIN. With 41 illustrations. Illuminated cloth.

Alice's Adventures in Wonderland.
Retold in words of one syllable for young people. By Mrs. J. C. GORHAM. With many illustrations. Illuminated cloth.

Andersen's Fairy Tales.
(Selections.) Retold in words of one syllable for young people. By HARRIET T. COMSTOCK. With many illustrations. Illuminated cloth.

Bible Heroes.
Told in words of one syllable for young people. By HARRIET T. COMSTOCK. With many illustrations. Illuminated cloth.

Black Beauty.
Retold in words of one syllable for young people. By MRS. J. C. GORHAM. With many illustrations. Illuminated cloth.

Grimm's Fairy Tales.
(Selections.) Retold in words of one syllable. By JEAN S. REMY. With many illustrations. Illuminated cloth.

Gulliver's Travels.
Into several remote regions of the world. Retold in words of one syllable for young people. By J. C. G. With 32 illustrations. Illuminated cloth.

Life of Christ.
Told in words of one syllable for young people. By JEAN S. REMY. With many illustrations. Illuminated cloth.

Lives of the Presidents.
Told in words of one syllable for young people. By JEAN S. REMY. With 24 large portraits. Illuminated cloth.

Pilgrim's Progress.
Retold in words of one syllable for young people. By SAMUEL PHILLIPS DAY. With 32 illustrations. Illuminated cloth.

Reynard the Fox:
The Crafty Courtier. Retold in words of one syllable for young people. By SAMUEL PHILLIPS DAY. With 23 illustrations. Illuminated cloth.

Robinson Crusoe.
His life and surprising adventures retold in words of one syllable for young people. By MARY A. SCHWACOFER. With 32 illustrations. Illuminated cloth.

Sanford and Merton.
Retold in words of one syllable for young people. By MARY GODOLPHIN. With 20 illustrations. Illuminated cloth.

Swiss Family Robinson.
Retold in words of one syllable for young people. Adapted from the original. With 32 illustrations. Illuminated cloth.

For sale by all booksellers, or sent postpaid on receipt of price by the publishers, A. L. BURT COMPANY, 114-120 East 23rd Street, New York.

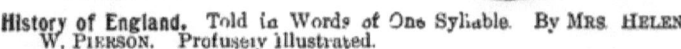